Robert Swindells left school at the age of fifteen and joined
the Royal Air Force at $17^1/_2$. After his discharge, he worked
at a variety of jobs, before training and working as a teacher.
He is now a full-time writer and lives with his wife Brenda
on the Yorkshire Moors. Robert Swindells has written many
books for young people, and in 1984 was the winner of the
Children's Book Award and the Other Award for his novel
Brother in the Land. He won the Children's Book Award for a
second time in 1990 with *Room 13*, and in 1994 *Stone Cold*
won the Carnegie Medal and the Sheffield Children's Book
Award.

UNBELIEVER

ROBERT SWINDELLS

PUFFIN BOOKS

PUFFIN BOOKS

Published by the Penguin Group
Penguin Books Ltd, 27 Wrights Lane, London W8 5TZ, England
Penguin Books USA Inc., 375 Hudson Street, New York, New York 10014, USA
Penguin Books Australia Ltd, Ringwood, Victoria, Australia
Penguin Books Canada Ltd, 10 Alcorn Avenue, Toronto, Ontario, Canada M4V 3B2
Penguin Books (NZ) Ltd, 182–190 Wairau Road, Auckland 10, New Zealand

Penguin Books Ltd, Registered Offices: Harmondsworth, Middlesex, England

First published by Hamish Hamilton 1995
Published in Puffin Books 1997
1 3 5 7 9 10 8 6 4 2

Copyright © Robert Swindells, 1995
All rights reserved

The moral right of the author has been asserted

Filmset in Bembo

Made and printed in England by Clays Ltd, St Ives plc

This book is for Margaret Clark and Jane Nissen

One

She isn't going to die. She *isn't*. He slipped the car keys in the pocket of his raincoat, turned up the collar and walked through the drizzle with his head down. The doors of the Citadel stood open, emitting a fuzzy incandescence which seemed to draw people as a flame draws moths.

Perhaps it was the sign which attracted them. The word **CITADEL** formed a pink arc.over a flickering blue cross. He paused, watching them enter. Most faces were familiar, though he noticed a few strangers. The Little Children. He smiled wryly. There *were* some children, but the congregation was mostly adult, and some members were well into middle age.

The stream of arrivals thinned, then ceased. There was just the light now, with drizzle slanting through it. He stepped into the porch and shrugged off his coat, savouring these last seconds of solitude. The Little Children were kindness itself and he knew he was in all of their prayers, but it was *his* wife who was dying, and all the sympathy in the world couldn't dispel the dread that shrouded his days. In fact, he sometimes found their sympathy unbearable, though he was reluctant to admit this to himself.

He hung his coat on a peg beside a pair of inner doors which stood open. Above these doors in golden capitals was a text. EXCEPT YE BE CONVERTED AND BECOME AS LITTLE CHILDREN YE SHALL NOT ENTER INTO THE KINGDOM OF HEAVEN. He paused, reading the words for perhaps the hundredth time before passing into the body of the hall. EXCEPT YE BE CONVERTED. Yes well, I *am*. I *am* converted. I've let Jesus into my life and in a few days' time I'll be baptised. That's enough, surely? He works miracles, doesn't He? He works them here, in this hall. I've *seen* them. He won't let her die. I know He won't.

Praise the Lord.

Two

'Annabel?'

'Yes, Mum?'

'Don't forget to iron a blouse for school tomorrow, will you?'

'No, Mum. I'll do it when I've wiped these few dishes. Shall I do one for Sarah, too?'

'If you wouldn't mind, dear. If I didn't feel so tired all the time —'

'It's okay, Mum. You rest. It's not a problem.'

The woman sighed, letting her head fall back on the cushion. Seems I hardly leave this armchair any more, she thought, except to go to bed. She smiled. Thank God Annabel copes. Not like poor Malcolm, working weekends, staying at the office till all hours because he can't bear to look at me. What on *earth* will he do when . . . She closed her eyes. No use thinking about that. People get by. They *have* to, and that's all there is to it. She sighed again, falling into a doze.

Annabel dropped the last spoon in the cutlery drawer and hung up the tea towel. It was seven twenty-nine by the kitchen clock. If she hurried with the ironing she could be at Salvo's for half eight. She'd told Tim eight o'clock, thinking Dad might be here to do the dishes but he was working late again. She sighed. If I was Mum, she mused, I'd be suspicious. Working late's a well-known alibi when a guy's got a bit on the side, isn't it? She unfolded the board, plugged in the iron and found two blouses in the airing cupboard.

She'd finished by a quarter to eight. She switched off the iron, unplugged it and stood it on the drainer to cool before carrying the blouses upstairs. Sarah was playing C.D.s in her room. Annabel poked her head round the door. 'There you go, kiddo – blouse for morning.' The younger girl nodded and smiled without removing the headphones. Annabel laid the garment on her sister's beside unit and went to her own room.

Old Sarah. Nothing gets to her. Wish *I* was eleven and she was fifteen, instead of the other way round. She brushed her hair, put on a bit of lipstick and dabbed Desert Flower behind her ears. She stood up and turned this way and that, looking at herself in the mirror. That'll have to do, she told herself.

Downstairs, she looked into the front room. Mum seemed to be sleeping. Reluctant to leave without a word she whispered 'Mum?' but her mother didn't stir. Annabel went through to the kitchen, scribbled a note on the pad, tore it off and left it on her mother's footstool. In the hallway she glanced at her watch. Eight exactly. With a bit of luck she'd make Salvo's by twenty past. She grabbed her jacket and bag and let herself out, blinking as the drizzle hit her face.

Three

'Do you know what life *is* for those people out there?' A sweep of the Pastor's arm indicated the world beyond the Citadel. 'Do you know what it *consists* of?' Nods and murmurs here and there in the congregation. 'Well, I'll tell you in one word. AP-PREHENSION.' The word was bellowed. It was left to hang on the air while the Pastor's eyes swept the rapt faces of his listeners. 'App-re-hen-sion.' He smiled wryly. 'A word of four syllables – one for each of the Gospels.' A ripple of mirth. 'A word of four syllables meaning FEARFUL ANTICIPA-TION.'

A fervent 'Yes, Lord!' came from somewhere near the front.

'Fearful anticipation.' The Pastor leaned forward over the lectern. 'Of what?' The words were spoken so quietly that Malcolm Henshaw found himself straining to hear. 'Of what?' The preacher straight-ened up, gripping the edges of his lectern. 'Of countless things. Of DEBT. Of UNEMPLOY-MENT. Of STROKE and HEART ATTACK, CANCER AND AIDS!' He bent over the lectern again. 'We *fear* these things, and yet we needn't. We live most of our lives in fearful anticipation of

misfortune, disease and death, and yet we needn't.'
He came out from behind the lectern, moving
slowly, pulling a white handkerchief from a pocket
of his grey suit to dab his brow while the congregation waited. Taking his time, he refolded the handkerchief and returned it to his pocket. A faint smile
played about the corners of his mouth. He looked
up.

'Did you ever hear of a little child worrying
about debt?'

'Lord, no.'

'Did you ever know a little child to live in fearful
anticipation of heart attack, stroke or Aids?'

'No, Lord.'

'Has anybody here met a little child whose every
day was haunted by his fear of cancer?'

'No, no.'

'OF COURSE YOU HAVEN'T. And why?
Because there's NO SUCH CHILD, that's why.
And WHY is there no such child? Because little
children don't FORNICATE. Don't DRINK.
Don't paint their FACES and go to all night parties.
Because little children don't ABUSE DRUGS or
lust after their neighbour's WIFE. In short, Brothers
and Sisters, little children are innocent of WRONG
LIVING!'

At these words the Citadel erupted in cries of
Alleluia and Praise the Lord. Worshippers raised
their right arms and waved them about in an ecstasy
of affirmation. The Pastor produced the handkerchief again, dabbing his forehead as he smiled down

from the dais. Malcolm Henshaw smiled and nodded, gazing at the preacher through a blur of grateful tears, wondering why he ever let things get on top of him. It was all so beautifully simple he wished everybody in the world was here to share it.

Four

'What flippin' time d'you call *this*?' said Tim, twisting in his seat to look up at her.

Annabel pulled a face. 'Sorry, Tim. My mum's bad again.'

'Ah, well!' He patted the empty chair beside him. 'Better late than never, I guess. Coke, is it?'

'Please.' The boy rose and went to the bar. Annabel smiled at the couple across the table. 'Hi, Celia, Rodney. Good weekend?'

Celia Buckley shrugged. 'Not bad.' Celia was Annabel's best friend.

'*I've* had a *fantastic* weekend.' Rodney Longstaff, class clown of Ten A at Meadway Comp, grinned. 'Saturday I got to go to *four* garden centres with my folks to buy plastic gnomes, and today my grandma came to lunch and Mum made her favourite – shepherd's pie.'

'Wheee!' cried Annabel. 'I don't know how you stand the excitement, Rod.'

Rodney shrugged. 'It just rolls off me, kid.'

Tim returned with her Coke. Salvo's did a terrific Coke. Tall frosted glass, lemon slice, lots of ice and two candy-stripe straws. Annabel clamped her mouth round the straws and sucked. Tim looked at

8

her. 'What exactly's *wrong* with your mum, Annabel?'

She relinquished the straws and shook her head. 'Uh-hu. Don't want to talk about it, Tim. Not here. This place is the only thing keeping me sane. Let's listen to the music, okay?'

Salvo's was Leyford's only nite spot. Monday through Saturday it catered for teens and twenties, serving alcohol and staying open till two in the morning. Sunday was Young Teens Nite – soft drinks, loud music, all over by ten. Annabel and Tim, Rod and Celia came every Sunday, sharing a table. Sharing a taxi, too, if it was wet, but pairing off for the walk home in dry weather.

They listened to the music, got up and danced, ordered more Cokes, listened to the music. It was still raining at five to ten so Rodney called a taxi. Annabel lived nearest so they dropped her off first. 'See you in school,' she grinned, provoking groans. She slammed the door and watched the vehicle roar off. As she turned to go through the gateway she saw the family Renault approaching, its headlamps turning the drizzle into a shoal of sparks.

Five

'Hi, Mum. Get my note, did you?'

Her mother smiled. 'Yes dear, I got it. I'm sorry I dozed off. Have you had fun?'

'Yes, thanks. Tim sends his love.'

'That's nice.' Her face clouded. 'I don't know what's happened to your dad – he's not been home.'

'He's coming. I saw the car as I got out of the taxi.'

'Oh, good.'

He came in while she was hanging up her jacket in the hallway.

'Foul night, sweetheart.'

'Yes.'

'Where've you been?'

'Salvo's.'

'Oh yes – Sunday, isn't it? I lose track of the days. Mum gone to bed?'

'No, she's on the settee, wondering if you'll be *sleeping* at the office next.'

'Is that what she *said*?'

'No. It's what *I'm* saying.'

'Don't be impertinent, Annabel.' He hung his coat next to hers and went into the front room. Annabel went through to the kitchen. Coke always made her thirsty. She drew a glass of water and stood by the sink, drinking it. She could hear her parents talking. Dad was probably telling Mum how he'd got involved with an important client and lost track of the time. Annabel shook her head. It's no *use*, Dad. She *knows* estate agents don't work Sundays – especially not till nine at night. You might as well come right out and *tell* her you'd rather shuffle bits of paper around in a deserted office than sit watching her fade away.

She was rinsing her glass when he came to put the kettle on. 'I'm making chocolate,' he said. 'Like a cup?'

'No thanks, I'm off to bed.' She put the glass on the drainer and picked up the iron. It was quite cold. She coiled its flex and put it away. Her father filled the kettle. 'Say goodnight to your mother before you go, won't you?'

'I always *do*, Dad.'

'And be quiet upstairs or you'll disturb your sister.'

'What d'you *think* I'm gonna do, Dad – put Millennium on?'

Millennium was her favourite band. Her father frowned. 'I told you before, Annabel – don't be impertinent. Impertinence to one's elders is a symptom of Wrong Living.'

Annabel looked at him. 'Wrong *living*? What the heck's *that*, for pete's sake?'

'You'll find out, young woman, soon enough.'

★

Annabel sat before the mirror in her room. Wrong living, she mumbled, wiping off the last trace of lipstick. That's a new one. Wonder where he got *that* from? Not the important client, that's for sure. Girlfriend? She balled up the Kleenex and dropped it in the waste-paper basket. Doubt it. She pulled a face. Who'd go out with *him*, anyway?

You'll find out soon enough. What was that – a threat? No. He was mad at me for cheeking him, that's all. It didn't mean anything. She winked at her reflection. Stop fussing, Annabel. Go to bed. Dream about Mig. Mig, Millennium's lead singer, grinned at her from the poster over the bed. She grinned back and kicked off her shoes.

Six

'Who's had a look at this?' The teacher pointed to the string she'd stretched diagonally across the classroom just above head height. A few hands went up. 'Anybody know what it is – yes, Rodney?'

'Piece of string, Miss.' Titters from Rodney's fans. Ms Channing sighed. 'Yes, Rodney, we know it's a piece of string but does anybody know what it's *for*? What are these, d'you think?' She tweaked one of the small rectangles of coloured card fastened at intervals to the string with paperclips. Along most of the line the cards were few and far between, but at one end there were many crowded together. Each card had something printed on it in black felt pen.

'Miss,' volunteered Annabel, 'it's a sort of calendar going back millions of years, with like important dates on it.'

The teacher nodded. 'That's right, Annabel. It's called a time line and its purpose is to help us imagine the vast period of time the Earth has existed, and how very recently the first hominids appeared.'

'Miss?'

'Yes, Timothy?'

'What's a hominid, Miss?'

'A hominid is a man-like creature, Timothy. There were many types of hominid, and one of them gave rise to modern man. The others proved defective or inadequate in one way or another and so they died out.'

'*I* didn't, Miss,' grinned Rodney.

The teacher gazed at him. 'Not yet, Rodney, but if you remain defective and inadequate I might be driven to lend evolution a hand.'

As the class laughed at this, a girl raised her hand. 'Miss – what about Adam and Eve?'

'What about them, Bronwen?'

'Well, Miss – were they hominids, or what?'

The teacher looked at her. 'Do you go to church, Bronwen?'

'Yes, Miss.'

'And what does your Minister say about Adam and Eve?'

'Miss, he's never mentioned them while I've been there. It's mostly New Testament at our church.'

Ms Channing nodded. 'Yes, well you see, most people today – mainstream Christians if you like – recognise that the story of Adam and Eve is a creation myth – a story invented in ancient times by the Hebrews to explain how the world began. Other cultures had their own creation myths and some of them are very beautiful, but none is widely believed nowadays.'

Bronwen nodded. The teacher turned and wrote *4,500,000,000 – formation of Earth's crust* on the board. Rodney Longstaff combed this for humorous inspiration, failed to find any and copied it into his jotter. Outside, a blustery wind flung drizzle at the window.

Seven

'What the heck's *sequestered* mean?'

'Where – let's see.' Annabel moved closer, squinting at the paperback Celia was reading as the pair walked home. 'Stop a minute – the print's going up and down.' Celia stopped and Annabel read aloud. ' "There once lived in a sequestered part of the county of Devonshire . . ." ' She shook her head. 'No idea. What book *is* it, anyway?'

Celia showed her friend the cover. '*Nicholas Nickleby*, you mammal – it's the set book for G.C.S.E.'

'You mean I've got to read *that*?' Annabel eyed the fat volume. 'Look how *thick* it is, for pete's sake – must be hundreds of pages.'

Celia turned to the back and flicked forward through the notes.

'Nine hundred and thirty-four.'

'Good grief! How far've you got?'

'Half-way down page fifty-nine.'

'God – you must be keen.'

Celia grinned. 'Not really. There's fifty-eight pages of introduction and I haven't bothered with that.'

'Turkey!'

Celia stuffed the book in her bag. 'Doing anything thrilling tonight, then?'

Annabel shrugged. 'Dunno. I've got to call at Tesco's and get something for tea, then cook it. I might have to wash up after and do a bit of hoovering, too – depends how Mum's been today.'

Celia looked at her friend. 'Your mum – is she going to get better or what? It's been a long time.'

Annabel shook her head. 'I don't think she'll get better. Dad seems to. He's forever on about things we'll do when Mum's well again.'

'Maybe he's pretending for Sarah.'

'No, he's pretending for *himself*, Celia. You only have to look at Mum to see she's getting worse, so Dad doesn't look.'

'How awful for you, Annabel. I think you're *ever* so brave.'

'No, I'm not. I'm terrified. I can't begin to imagine what'll become of us – you know – after.' She smiled briefly. 'A nine-hundred-page book's just what I need right now.'

Celia didn't know how to respond to this, and the two walked on in silence till their ways divided. Annabel punched her friend's arm. 'Hey – see you tomorrow?'

'Sure will.' Celia began to turn away, then stopped. 'Hey listen, Annabel – you're my best friend, right? If – you know – if you ever want to talk —' She pulled a face. 'Well – you know what I mean.'

Annabel nodded. 'I know. Thanks.'

Eight

'So, Annabel.' Her father gazed at her across the table. 'What did you do at school today?' Annabel, toying with her quiche, shrugged. 'Nothing.'

'Oh, come on. It's September, a new school year's getting under way and you did nothing?'

Annabel sighed. 'Kids don't like talking about school, Dad. It's boring.' She looked at him. 'Did you know the Earth's crust was formed four thousand, five hundred million years ago?'

'No, I didn't. Four thousand, five hundred million.' He shook his head. 'I don't see how that can be, Annabel, considering we *know* God created the world about six *thousand* years ago.'

Annabel snorted. 'And did you know *Nicholas Nickleby* has nine hundred and thirty-four pages and I've got to read every one of 'em and some Shakespeare too?'

Her father looked at her. 'Why did you make that dismissive noise when I mentioned the Creation, Annabel?'

She shrugged. 'I assumed you were joking, Dad.'

'We're doing about hunger,' interrupted Sarah, sensing conflict. Her father looked at her. 'Hunger?'

'Yes, you know – in Africa and India. Famine and drought. What causes them.'

'And what *does* cause them, Sarah?'

'I don't know *yet*, Dad – we just started today.'

'*I* can tell you. Part of it, anyway.'

'What, then?'

'Wrong living.'

Oh-oh, thought Annabel. Here it comes again. Sarah frowned.

'What's *that* mean, Dad?'

'Well – it means people live in a bad way, Sarah, and that makes things go wrong in their lives.'

Annabel looked across at him. 'So Africans and Indians do more bad things than we do?'

Her father shook his head. 'I didn't say that, Annabel. They have hunger, we suffer from other things. Perhaps if we behaved differently all these things would disappear.'

'But famine's often caused by locusts or lack of rain. Those things aren't affected by anything *we* do.'

'How do you *know*, Annabel? The plague of locusts in the Bible came because of what Pharaoh was doing to the Israelites.'

'That's a *story*, Dad. Nobody knows if it really happened.'

'Of *course* they do – it says so in the Bible.'

'Sure. And we know if we go down a rabbit hole we find ourselves in another world because it says so in Alice in Wonderland.'

'You surely don't mean to compare —?'

'Yes, Dad, I mean to compare. A book's a book.

Something doesn't become true just because it's in print. Excuse me.' She pushed back her chair, got up and left the room.

Nine

'Frayle.' Mr Cordingley skimmed the essay onto Tim's desk. 'Frail, Frayle. Very frail. Buckley – the same. Pearce – the less said the better. Longstaff —' He paused, holding Rodney's paper by a corner as though he'd just fished it out of the lavatory. 'You were asked to write a fragment of autobiography. You certainly wrote a fragment – I needed an electron microscope to *find* it, and when I did it turned out to be about your C.D. collection. You do know what autobiography *means*, I take it?'

'Yessir. It's like, your life story written by yourself.'

'Exactly.' He let the paper fall onto the boy's desk. 'Do it again, and let it be crammed with sparkling incident.'

'Sir, nothing's ever happened in *my* life.'

'Something *will*, Longstaff, if your piece is not on my desk first thing in the morning.'

Nobody tittered. Nobody ever did in Mr Cordingley's classes. Mr Cordingley was head of English, and a teacher of the old school. No first names for him. If your surname was Smith, then as far as Mr Cordingley was concerned you were Smith. He'd no more dream of calling you Karen or Darren or whatever than you would of calling him Roderick. Behind his back however, he was Old Rod to every pupil at Meadway Comp and always had been.

'Henshaw.' He beamed down on Annabel. 'You have the divine gift of the storyteller, young woman, though your life seems almost to parallel that of Madeline Bray, a character in the novel we shall study this term. Well done.' He handed the paper to Annabel, who blushed and lowered her eyes. She hated being singled out in class.

The teacher passed on, dispensing essays like a gambler dealing cards. When he'd finished he went out to the front and wrote on the board, *The moving machinery exists only to display static characters.* Turning to the class he said, 'Who can tell me who wrote that?' Rodney's hand went up. 'Yes, Longstaff?'

'You, Sir.' Rodney glanced about him, looking for mirth in the faces of his fans. None showed.

'Come out here, boy.' He got up and walked out to the front. The teacher thrust his face into the boy's till their noses almost touched. He spoke so quietly nobody could hear except Rodney, but the boy never doubted his sincerity. 'There are no clowns in my classes, Longstaff. Here, laughter is an occasional indulgence inspired by great comic literature and led by myself. If you aspire to the life of a clown I strongly advise you to run away and join a circus. If not, you will confine yourself to the role of pupil and leave comedy to those who do it well. Have I made myself quite clear?'

'Yessir.'

'Good.' Old Rod took his face away and Rodney returned to his place.

Ten

Tuesday, twenty-five past seven. Malcolm Henshaw parked at the kerb and went into the Citadel. His family thought he was working late, and this was one of several things which were worrying him – one of the points he meant to raise tonight with the Pastor.

Why secrecy? If what he was doing was right (and it *was*, of course it was) why hadn't he told Suzanne? He'd been coming here three times a week for almost three months, yet nobody at home had any idea that he'd been saved. Soon he would undergo baptism – be born again, but could it be right to take this momentous step without the knowledge of his wife and children?

He knew the answer, of course, deep down, just as he knew why he hadn't taken Suzanne into his confidence. He was afraid. Afraid she'd scoff. You wouldn't know to look at her now, but Suzanne was a strong woman with definite views. On balance she was a lover of humanity, but there were one or two things she despised and fundamentalism was one of them. There was absolutely no chance of Suzanne's grudging acquiescence to what he was about to do, let alone her blessing. Malcolm knew this and it hurt, because after all he was doing it for her.

And of course the Pastor didn't know. He'd explained that Suzanne was too ill to come here, and everybody assumed that was why she stayed away. Will it change things, he wondered, when they know about Suzanne's views? Will they still want me? Might the Pastor refuse me baptism?

These were thorny questions and they had to be resolved. Now. Tonight. These twice-weekly meetings were usually devoted to Bible Study, but when a baptism was imminent the candidate was expected to voice any qualms he might be feeling, and to ask for the prayers of those present.

The big room was bare, its chairs stacked round the walls. Its only occupant was Andrew, the eight-year-old son of Lynn and Stephen, who must have gone through to the small room where Bible Study was conducted. The child smiled at Malcolm. 'Good evening, Brother.'

'Oh – er – hello, Andrew. Has everybody gone through?'

'All except you, Brother Malcolm.' He grinned. 'You look scared. Are you?'

Malcolm pulled a face. 'Nervous.'

'There's no need, Brother. Jesus loves you.'

'Yes, I know. Where are your friends tonight?'

The boy shrugged. 'They didn't come, but that's all right. We're never alone when we're saved.'

'Er – no, I suppose not.' The child's precocity

made him uncomfortable. 'Well.' He smiled tightly. 'Better go in, eh? I'll see you later, Andrew.'

'I'll be praying for you, Brother.'

Eleven

Wednesday morning, first period. Geography. Rodney Longstaff stuck his hand up. 'Miss?'

The teacher sighed. 'Yes, Rodney?' She anticipated a diversionary tactic and she was right.

'You know educational trips, Miss – like when last year's Ten A were doing *Jane Eyre* and old – and Mr Cordingley took them all to Haworth to see where Charlotte Brontë lived?'

'Yes, I remember. What about it, Rodney?'

'Well, Miss – it's *Nicholas Nickleby* this year and all we're doing is going to some boring old museum to look at a Victorian schoolroom.'

Ms Channing pulled a face. 'That's hard luck, Rodney, but I fail to see what it has to do with what we're doing here this morning.'

'Oh, but it has, Miss.' Rodney pointed to the time line. 'There's a card about dinosaurs on there, Miss. It says: *220,000,000 – dinosaurs appear in fossil record*. I read it just now.'

'That's right, Rodney – we'll come to dinosaurs later this term.'

'Well, Miss – *Jurassic Park*'s on at the Odeon this week and next. You could take us, Miss – it'd be *dead* educational, and it'd make up for us not having a proper English trip.'

A mixed chorus of assent and dinosaur noises greeted this suggestion. The teacher waited, smiling faintly till it subsided, then spoke. 'Rodney Longstaff, I suspect you know very well there isn't the slightest chance of the Governors forking out a hundred and fifty pounds so that Ten A can see *Jurassic Park* for nothing *and* miss half a day's work, but I congratulate you on an ingenious attempt to delay the start of this lesson. Now – may we continue, or have you another trick up your sleeve?'

The boy grinned and shook his head. 'That's it for now, Miss.'

'Good. Then we'll look at the earliest evidence of life – fossil blue-green algae.'

'Oooh, goody!' murmured Rodney.

Tim found Annabel by the bikesheds at morning break. 'Hey, Annabel – a bunch of us're off to see *Jurassic* tomorrow night – fancy coming?'

Annabel nodded. 'Sure, if I can get away. Who's going?'

'Rodney, Simon, Bronwen. One or two others. Celia'll come if you ask her.'

'Okay.'

'Seven o'clock, then, outside the Odeon?'

'Right.'

Twelve

Thursday, six o'clock. The Henshaws at their meal. It's *Pasta Joke*, a dish consisting of macaroni and tuna in a tomato sauce, created and christened by Annabel.

'Dad?'

'Yes, sweetheart?'

'Some of the kids're off to the Odeon tonight. *Jurassic Park*. I've arranged to meet 'em at seven.'

'Oh.' He glanced at his wife, then down at his plate. 'It's a bit inconvenient, Annabel. I'm going out myself and your mother's not feeling well. Can't you go tomorrow?'

'Sure, if I want to go all by myself. The kids're off *tonight*, Dad.'

'It's all right.' Suzanne laid her knife and fork on her plate and pushed it away. She'd hardly touched her food. 'I feel much better now. You go, both of you. Sarah and I will be fine watching T.V.'

'Hmmm.' Malcolm Henshaw continued to gaze at his plate. 'I'd rather you had Annabel too, Suzanne, and I'm not sure she ought to go, anyway.'

Suzanne looked at him. 'Whyever not, dear? She'll be with her friends. She's done it many times before.'

'Yes, I know, but that doesn't mean it's a good idea.' He looked at Annabel. 'I suppose there'll be boys in the group?'

'Yes, Dad, there'll be boys. You know them. Tim. Rodney. Boys in my class.'

He nodded. 'I know them, and I'm asking you not to go. I'm not *telling*, sweetheart, I'm asking. Will you stay with your mother?'

'Da-ad.' Annabel looked down, her underlip caught between her teeth. It was so unfair. What could she say when he put it like that? What could she *possibly* say? No, I *won't* stay with my mother – I know she's dying but my friends are more important to me? No, of course not. He'd put her in an impossible position so he could go out himself. At that moment she hated her father. Hated him. She looked up, fighting back tears. 'Okay, I'll stay, but they'll give me hell at school tomorrow. I *promised* I'd be there.'

Her father smiled briefly. 'If they do *that* sweetheart, they're not worth having as friends. *Real* friends stick by you through thick and thin.'

Annabel looked away from him. Real husbands do too, she thought, but didn't say.

Thirteen

'Ah – Malcolm.' The Pastor rose beaming as Malcolm entered the room. The ten occupants of the hard chairs smiled. Malcolm smiled back and took the one vacant seat.

'Now, Brother.' The Pastor gazed at him. 'You know everybody here, and each of them has been through what you are going through now. We're on your side, so do speak freely. There may be some little thing – something which cropped up in Bible Study perhaps – which you're not completely happy about, or it might be something completely different. It doesn't matter.' He smiled. 'Whatever it is, you may be sure we've met with it before and dealt with it through prayer and meditation.'

The ten nodded. 'Alleluia,' mumbled Lynn. 'Praise the Lord,' said Neil. They were all looking at Malcolm. He felt his cheeks burn. 'Well ...' Keeping his eyes fixed on the dingy linoleum between his feet, he told them about Suzanne's antipathy towards fundamentalism. He confessed to having deceived his family for three months in order to attend meetings. He told them he was unhappy about this, and asked them to tell him what he must do.

The Pastor, whose name was Ken, smiled and told him he must eliminate Wrong Living. He must eliminate it in his own life by revealing the good news of his salvation to his family, and in his family's lives by insisting on standards of conduct consistent with the teachings of the Bible. 'You cannot compel your children to let Jesus into their lives,' he said, 'but you *can* and *must* protect them from Satan's snares, which are all around.' Malcolm asked for an example and the preacher said, 'Evolution. The *theory* of evolution, which is taught as though it were a fact.' He looked at Malcolm. 'How d'you think a mere theory's caught on like that, Brother?'

Malcolm shrugged. 'Fossils, I suppose. Dinosaur bones. Flint arrowheads, cave paintings. It seems sort of obvious there were animals we don't have now. People, too.'

'Obvious, yes. And do you know *why* it seems so obvious? Do you know why all these clues exist – why they haven't mouldered away over the centuries?'

'Not really, no.'

'Because they're not what they seem. They haven't *been* there centuries. They're artefacts placed in the earth by Satan to mislead humanity.'

Are they? Are they really? He sat motionless on the edge of his seat, hands on knees, staring at the floor, thinking, can you *prove* that, or is it another theory? Pastor Ken had picked up a Bible – not to read from but to brandish. He was holding it high, shaking it, saying something about Genesis. Malcolm listened with half his mind. With the other half he was imagining Satan in a cave somewhere at this very moment, painting buffaloes on the wall.

Fourteen

'You *go* Annabel,' insisted Suzanne. 'Sarah'll make me the odd cuppa, won't you darling?'

Sarah nodded, smiling. 'We'll have a better time without you, anyway.'

'Cheeky!' Annabel aimed a swipe at her sister's head, missing on purpose. 'I'll go, then. *I* know when I'm not wanted.'

There were eight for *Jurassic Park*. Afterwards they split into two groups of four. Annabel went with Tim, Celia and Rodney to McDonald's. It was a quarter to ten.

'So what d'you reckon?' asked Tim as they settled round a table with their orders. 'Good, or what?'

'Terrific,' said Annabel. 'I think old Channing should see it – liven her up a bit.'

'I think she should be *in* it,' grinned Rodney. 'She was a young lass in those days, you know.'

'What *I* think,' put in Celia, 'is that the four of us should get together when we leave school and open Blue Green Algae Park. Channing can do conducted tours while we sit in the office counting the dosh.'

They ate and talked and slurped Coke. At ten

o'clock Annabel said, 'I'd better go. Sarah's on her own with Mum.'

Rodney looked at her. 'Your mum eat kids or something?'

Annabel shook her head. 'She's ill. If she collapsed, Sarah wouldn't know what to do.'

'Would *you*?'

Tim flashed Rodney a look. 'Lay off, you div.' He smiled at Annabel. 'See you tomorrow, then.'

She looked at him. 'Aren't you coming?'

'Not *yet*, Annabel. It's only five past ten, and anyway I haven't finished my Coke.'

'Celia?'

The girl shook her head. 'You go on, Annabel. I'm not ready.' She avoided Annabel's gaze.

'Okay.' She stood up. 'I'll see you in school if I don't get murdered on the way home.'

They all laughed.

Fifteen

'Hi, Mum. Sarah in bed?'

'Just gone up.'

'You been all right?'

'Fine, dear, thanks. How was the film?'

Annabel was about to answer when her father came through from the kitchen. 'So you went out after all, Annabel?'

Annabel nodded. 'Mum said it was all right and Sarah couldn't wait to get rid of me. How was *your* outing?'

'Fine, thanks.' He handed his wife a mug and sat down with his own. 'Your mother asked about the film.'

'Yes. *Jurassic Park*. It was terrific, thanks. I'm glad I didn't miss it.'

'It's about dinosaurs, isn't it?'

'That's right. They find this fossil insect in a bit of amber and use its DNA to recreate dinosaurs.'

'All nonsense, of course.'

Annabel shrugged. 'Science fiction based on fact, Dad. They *have* found insects in amber, millions of years old.'

Her father smiled. 'They *think* they have.'

'No, they have. It's a scientific fact.'

'That's what we're *supposed* to believe, Annabel, and most people do, but they're wrong.'

'So what are they if they aren't fossilised insects, Dad? You tell me.'

'They're artefacts placed in the earth by Satan to mislead us.'

Mother and daughter looked at him. 'Where on earth did you get *that* from, Malcolm?' asked his wife.

Malcolm smiled. 'A man I was talking to this evening, Suzanne. A Pastor.'

'A Pastor? Was he looking for a house or something?'

'No, no. He was conducting a class. A Bible class.'

'You went to a *Bible* class?'

He smiled. 'I've been going for months, darling. I didn't tell you because I'm familiar with your views on fundamentalism.'

'You ... you've been attending *fundamentalist* classes all this time and pretending you were occupied with business?'

'I *was* occupied with business, Suzanne. God's business.'

'And this Pastor,' interrupted Annabel, 'he told you Satan fakes fossil insects?'

'Yes. Fossils in general.'

'And you believe him?'

'I don't know, sweetheart. I'm thinking about it.'

Annabel shook her head. 'And you say *Jurassic Park*'s nonsense?'

Malcolm smiled. 'I have let Jesus into my life, Annabel, and I can't tell you what a difference it has made.' He gazed at her.

'Only one thing is needed to make my happiness complete.'

'Oh, yes – what?'

'That you and Sarah should let Him into your lives, too.'

'No way. Not me, anyhow. Not the way *you* mean. Sarah can please herself.'

'No!' Suzanne shook her head. 'Sarah's not *old* enough to please herself.' She looked at her husband. 'I don't know why you've got yourself involved with this – this *sect*, whatever it is, but . . .'

'The Little Children,' said Malcolm. 'They're called The Little Children.'

His wife shook her head. 'Whatever. I know I can't stop *you*, but I'm not having Sarah brain-washed. And don't look at me like *that*, Malcolm. I know how these people operate.'

Malcolm shook his head. 'You're tired, Suzanne. We'll talk tomorrow.' He smiled. 'I want to tell you all about the arrangements for my baptism.'

'You were baptised as a *baby*,' cried Suzanne. 'It isn't something that *wears off*, Malcolm. You're *in* the Church. You don't *need* some self-ordained little Bible-thumper shoving your head underwater – especially one who thinks the Devil's running a fossil factory. I'm going to bed.'

'Me too,' said Annabel. She turned in the door-way. '*You* know there were dinosaurs, Dad. You used to read to me from that dinosaur book I had when I was little. You can pretend till you're blue in the face – you and the other Little Children – but you'll *always* know, deep down. G'night.'

Sixteen

'That you, Annabel?'

'Yes.' She stuck her head round Sarah's door. 'Did you have a good time without me, then?'

'Sure did. Come here a minute.'

Annabel entered the dim room and sat on the edge of the bed. 'What?'

'Are Mum and Dad okay, Annabel?'

'How d'you mean?'

'They're not – breaking up or anything?'

'Breaking up? 'Course not, silly. What put *that* idea in your head?'

'Well – Dad goes out all the time and Mum looks fed up. I asked her where he was tonight and she said, you might well ask. I wondered if he'd got – you know – a girl-friend.'

'No, you turkey!' She ruffled her sister's hair. 'He's sniffing round one of these religious sects.'

'Religious sex?'

'Sects. S-E-C-T-S. The Little Children, they call themselves. He's been to one of their meetings tonight.'

'Are they – sinister, d'you think?'

Annabel chuckled. 'I doubt whether they sacrifice babies if that's what you mean, but they think the

Devil plants fossils for scientists to find.'

'The Devil?'

'Yeah, you know – Satan.'

'Why would he do that?'

'Dad says, to mislead us.'

'Oh. What else do they believe?'

'I dunno, kid, but I've got a feeling Dad'll tell us soon enough.' She stood up. 'Anyway it's nothing for you to worry about so go to sleep. See you in the morning.'

'Okay. G'night, Annabel.'

'Night, Sarah. Sweet dreams.'

Seventeen

'Okay.' Mr Bickford's tone was as bright as the eyes with which he regarded Ten A that Friday morning. He was a thin young man with a slight stoop and the sparse, receding hair which had earned him his nickname. Baldy Bickford. He rubbed his slim, dry hands together. 'Since this is our first session together, I thought we'd give it a sort of introductory format.' He smiled. 'That way I get to know you, you get to know me and we all get a rough idea of what we'll be covering in R.E. leading up to the exam next June.'

Muffled groans greeted the word exam. This was Ten A's G.C.S.E. year, and everything from now on would be geared towards the dreaded exams. The teacher smiled again. 'There's no reason why every one of you shouldn't pass with at least a B, so don't worry. It's my aim to make the course enjoyable as well as arduous. Now – how many of you attend a church or other place of worship?'

A few hands went up. Mr Bickford counted. 'Eight of you. Okay, thanks. That leaves eighteen who don't. How many of the eighteen *believe* in something? Yes, Rodney – what do you believe in?'

'Fairies, sir.' Laughter rippled round the room.

'Fairies.' The teacher looked at him. 'Have you actualy *seen* fairies, Rodney?'

'No, sir. Have you seen God?'

Mr Bickford sighed. 'Look Rodney, that's a fair question, but I don't want us to get into a deep philosophical discussion this morning. I'm not ducking the issue – we *will* talk about this later, but just for now let's keep it fairly simple, okay?'

'Yessir.'

'Right. So seventeen of us believe in nothing at all, is that right?' Annabel raised her hand.

'Yes, Annabel?'

'I believe in dinosaurs, sir.'

'Look.' Mr Bickford sighed again. 'We're talking about religion here. Our religious beliefs, or lack of them. Fairies and dinosaurs *will* come into our discussions at some stage, but not today. All right, Annabel?'

'Sir, I mentioned it because my dad doesn't.'

'Doesn't what, Annabel?'

'Believe in dinosaurs, sir. He says fossils are artefacts placed in the earth by Satan to mislead mankind.'

'Ah.' The teacher nodded. 'I take it your father's a Christian, Annabel?'

'I think so, sir.'

'What denomination?'

'I don't know, sir. He's started going to something called The Little Children.'

Mr Bickford nodded. 'A fundamentalist sect. And you're not a member yourself?'

'No, sir, just my dad. I think it's weird, sir.'

'Yes, well.' The teacher looked down, choosing his words. 'Christian fundamentalists believe the Bible to be holy writ, Annabel. That means every word of the Bible is literally true, including Genesis. And if the story of Adam and Eve is true, evolution *can't* be.'

'Ms Channing says Adam and Eve's a creation myth, sir.'

'Yes, Annabel. That's the generally accepted view today, but fundamentalists reject it for the reason I mentioned.'

'But what do *you* think, sir? About fossils, I mean. *Were* there dinosaurs?'

Mr Bickford shook his head. 'I'd prefer not to answer that, Annabel. Not now. Not in class. If you want to talk to me privately about it I'm usually available at break-times and after school.' He glanced around the class. 'The same applies to each of you, of course. Now – where were we?'

Eighteen

She'd decided not to mention Mr Bickford's lesson for fear of starting her father off, but over tea her mother said, 'Wasn't it today you were finding out what you'll be doing in R.E. this year, Annabel?'

Annabel sighed. September, and Mum was panicking about G.C.S.E. already. She nodded. 'We're doing Comparative Religion, Mum.' She speared a piece of haddock and put it in her mouth, hoping Mum would leave it at that.

'Comparative Religion – that's learning about other faiths, isn't it? We did a bit of that at *my* school.' She smiled. 'I remember they took us round a mosque and Teresa Parsons was sent out for putting a hanky over her nose and mouth and doing a belly-dance. It was a revolutionary new idea in those days, of course.'

'What – belly-dancing?'

'No, dear. Comparative Religion.'

'Load of nonsense,' growled Malcolm. 'We did Christianity, Christianity and Christianity at *my* school, and you should be doing the same, Annabel. It's the true religion, after all.'

His wife looked at him. 'You can't *say* that, Malcolm. Everybody believes their religion to be the true one. Maybe they're *all* true.'

'How can they all be true?' He was eating peas. One flew out of his mouth and landed in the sauce boat. Sarah giggled. 'There's only one God, and He *hasn't* got six arms or a head like an elephant.'

'How d'you know?' asked Annabel. 'Have you seen Him? Come to that, how do you know it's a He? Why not a She?'

Her father sighed. 'Feminism she chucks at me now. Does *that* count as a religion these days – I wouldn't be surprised.'

'Why not? Makes more sense than fundamentalism. Mr Bickford says The Little Children is a fundamentalist sect. He says they believe every word of the Bible is literally true – even Adam and Eve.'

Malcolm arched his brow. 'Sounds as though he was poking fun, Annabel. Was he?'

Annabel shook her head. 'No way. He just said they believe the Bible to be literally true so they can't accept evolution, and when I asked what *he* thought about fossils and that, he wouldn't say. Told me to see him by myself if I wanted to talk about that.'

'Did he now? Well you're *not* to, Annabel, understand?' He punctuated his words with his knife, little stabbing motions. 'If you want to talk about The Little Children, come to me. I'm not having your head stuffed with rubbish by somebody who doesn't know what he's talking about.'

Annabel looked down at her plate. Who put the

fun in fundamentalism, she thought. She wanted to say it, but didn't. She scraped the last sliver of fish from its skin and impaled it on her fork.

Nineteen

Ten o'clock Saturday morning, Annabel met Celia by arrangement at the Mall. The Mall was Leyford's shopping centre. It was circular, a great wheel of gleaming marble, whose concourses radiated from the hub like spokes. At the hub, under the soaring glass dome of the roof, stood Island. Island was a coffee shop with a cascade and living trees. It was said that if you sat there long enough you'd see everyone in Leyford. Celia had got there before her.

'Hi, Celia.'

'Hi, Annabel. What d'you want to do first?'

Annabel put her coffee on the table and sat down. 'Look in Smith's, I suppose. Get a copy of *Nicholas Nickleby*.' She looked at her friend. 'I suppose you're half-way through it by now?'

Celia shook her head. 'No way. I'm on chapter two.'

'What's it about?'

'Business, so far.'

'Oh, yippee! I can think of better ways to spend £4.99.'

'Yeah, well.'

They sipped their coffee. Celia watched the shoppers. Annabel gazed at the silver birches, wondering whether they missed the wind and the rain. Presently Celia said, 'Penny for 'em.'

'What?'

She smiled. 'Penny for 'em. Your thoughts. It's what my gran says when she catches me miles away.'

'Oh, right.' Annabel smiled. 'I was thinking about the trees. They were big when they were planted here, so they probably grew outside. D'you think they miss – you know – wind and rain and birds perching on 'em? I mean, it's like they're in *jail* or something, isn't it?'

Celia chuckled. 'You're a nut Annabel, d'you know that?' She looked towards the nearest tree. 'They're laughing, these trees. They've got it made. Think about it. No frost. No storms to wreck 'em. No caterpillars nibbling holes in their leaves. No birds crapping all over them. They're fed and watered and the security guys won't let you carve your initials in 'em. I'd *love* it here if I was a tree.'

Annabel shook her head. 'It's not *natural* though, is it?'

They strolled along to Smith's and looked under Classics. *Nicholas Nickleby* was there with some other Dickens stuff. Annabel pulled it out. 'You notice it's the thickest of the lot,' she growled. 'Just think. They chopped a tree down to make this.' She grinned. 'I'd rather have had the tree, wouldn't *you*?'

Celia looked at her. 'What *is* this – National Tree

Day or something?' She smiled. 'You're right, though. *I* wish they'd kept the tree.'

Annabel paid for the book, then stood by the till, leafing through it. Celia frowned. 'What're you looking for?'

'Madeline Bray. Old Rod said I was like her, remember? I want to see if he was insulting me or not.'

'Come *on*.' Celia tugged her sleeve. 'We're blocking the gangway. You could look all day and not find her. Anyway, I've got a better idea.'

Annabel closed the book, clucking when she found it wouldn't fit in her pocket. 'What?'

'We'll go to the library. Get the York Notes. Madeline Bray'll be easier to find and we can pinch some ideas for the exam.'

Annabel shrugged. 'Okay, genius, lead on.' They left the Mall and sauntered along Market Street, heading for the library.

Twenty

'Have you got the York Notes on *Nicholas Nickleby*, please?'

The library assistant nodded. 'You'll find it in the 823s, unless it's out.'

It wasn't out, but there was only one copy. The girls returned with it to the desk. 'Is this the only copy?' asked Celia.

The assistant nodded. 'I'm afraid so.' She smiled. 'Good move on your part to grab it now – they'll be queueing up for it next spring.'

'Why don't you get more copies, then?'

The woman shrugged. 'No money. You could always buy your own, of course.'

Celia grinned. 'No money.'

They sat at a table in the Quiet Room and Annabel found the commentary on Madeline Bray. It was just a few lines. 'Huh!' she went, when she'd read it.

Celia held out a hand. 'Let's see.' Annabel slid the book across and Celia read the worst bits out loud. '*A colourless character – virtual prisoner – completely passive – giving in totally to her father's will.*' She looked up, grinning. 'Sounds like you, Annabel. I don't know why I hang around with you, really.'

Annabel lunged forward across the table and took a swipe at her friend's head, missing on purpose. 'You can bog off if that's the way you feel.' She snatched the book and read the commentary again. 'Cheeky beggar!' she growled, referring to Mr Cordingley. 'Just because I wrote that I have a lot of jobs to do with Mum being ill.'

Celia smiled. 'He might have meant your artistic talent. It says she has some.'

'I doubt it, knowing Old Rod. Anyway, you won't catch *me* giving in totally to my father's will.'

'That's what I like to hear.' Celia stood up. 'Come on – let's get back to the Mall.'

'Who's going to have the book?'

'Me, of course, you colourless character. It's on my ticket.' She grinned. 'It'll be a good excuse for you to come over to my place in the evenings – we're forced to work together 'cause there's only one book.'

Annabel nodded. 'That's what *I* like to hear.'

They walked back to the Mall to browse through Body Shop and look at clothes and shoes.

Twenty-One

Sarah looked at her father. 'Where's Mum?'

He was laying strips of bacon on the grill. 'She's staying in bed for a while this morning.'

'Why?'

'Because it's Sunday and she's a bit tired. I'm doing her a breakfast tray. You can take it up if you like.'

'Yes, please.' She sat down and poured cornflakes into her bowl. Annabel came in, yawning. 'Where's Mum?'

'In bed,' said Sarah. 'Dad says I can take her breakfast up.'

Malcolm slid the pan under the grill. 'What are your plans for the day, Annabel?' She looked out of the window. It was drizzling. She shrugged. 'I've got English homework.'

'What is it?'

'We've got to read the first four chapters of *Nicholas Nickleby*.'

'Oh – reading.' He broke an egg into the pan. 'That's not work. I suppose you're going to that dreadful club this evening?'

'No.' She was giving Salvo's a miss because of the way Tim and the others had let her travel home alone last week. Not that they'd care. 'Why?'

'I'm going to church and I was thinking of taking Sarah.'

'Me?' said Sarah, surprised.

'She might not want to go,' said Annabel.

'She won't know till she's tried it. You'll come with your dad won't you, sweetheart?'

Sarah nodded. 'I suppose. Is Mum's tray ready yet?'

'Two minutes.'

After breakfast Annabel went upstairs. She was going to read in her room, but she popped her head round her mother's door first. Mum was lying back, propped on pillows with the tray across her thighs. She smiled. 'I'm having a lazy day, Annabel.'

Annabel looked at the tray. 'You've hardly touched your breakfast, Mum. Are you feeling okay?' She knew her mother would say yes, even if she wasn't.

'I'm fine, dear, but not very hungry. You can take the tray if you will.'

Dad was washing up. Annabel put the tray on the drainer. 'Mum's not hungry.'

'No.' He looked at the untouched food. 'She eats nothing these days. No wonder she's tired.'

Annabel said nothing. If he wanted to kid himself Mum was ill because she didn't eat instead of the other way round, that was his business.

In her room, she settled herself on the chair by the window and opened *Nicholas Nickleby*. Faintly through the wall she could hear one of Sarah's C.D.s playing. Lucky little beggar, she thought. Not a care in the world. Mind you, I don't envy her The Little Children. Not a million laughs there, I bet.

Twenty-Two

It was just after nine when Malcolm and Sarah got back from church. Annabel could tell her father was fired up. He couldn't keep still but paced the room, speaking more loudly than usual.

'It was electrifying, Suzanne. There's no other word for it. I *wish* you'd been there. That Pastor's inspired. Inspired.' Malcolm sat down on the sofa, then got up again. 'He said we accumulate too much baggage, only he wasn't talking about – you know – suitcases and carriers. He meant attitudes, Suzanne. Assumptions. Concerns. He said these things clog up our lives, blocking out more and more of the light till we can no longer see how beautiful the world is. He said we call that growing up. Children don't have that. They haven't accumulated this baggage so they see things as they really are, which is why they're always filled with wonder and curiosity.'

Suzanne looked at Sarah, who was untying her shoelaces. 'And did you enjoy yourself, darling?' Sarah looked up and shrugged.

'It was all right, Mum. Some bits were quite weird.'

'Weird? What d'you mean, darling?'

'She didn't understand, that's all,' interjected Malcolm. 'Some of it was a bit abstract. A bit philosophical.'

'Or maybe,' suggested Annabel, 'she was seeing things as they really are. You know – being a kid with no baggage and all.'

'You weren't there, Annabel,' growled her father. 'You know nothing about it.'

'I'm a bit tired,' said Sarah, to head off an argument. 'I think I'll go to bed if that's all right.'

Her mother smiled. 'Of course it's all right. Goodnight, darling.'

'Night, Mum. Night, Dad, Annabel.'

Annabel got up as her sister left the room. 'I'm making hot chocolate if anybody'd like some. Mum?'

'Oooh, yes, please, darling.' Things might blow over if Annabel left the room.

'Dad?'

'Might as well, since you're putting the kettle on.'

Ground glass, she thought in the kitchen. Two sugars for Mum, ground glass for Dad. She chuckled, replaying the words she'd stung him with. *Being a kid with no baggage and all*. Good, that. No answer to it.

Later, on her way to bed, she popped into Sarah's room. The light was out but her sister was awake. Annabel sat on the bed.

'Tell me about the weird stuff.'

Sarah yawned. 'It was nothing, really.' She shifted, clasping her hands behind her head. 'This woman. Pastor Ken's talking, right? And suddenly this woman jumps up and starts banging on, only she's not using real words. Talking gibberish, you know, but everyone thinks it's great. Pastor Ken goes praise the Lord, and then everybody's saying it – even Dad. You have to put your hand up when you say it, like this.'

'Like at school when you need to go to the toilet?'

'Yes.' Sarah giggled. 'Anyway, she goes on for a bit, then sits down suddenly. Slumps on the chair, and two or three people rush to hold her up. I was a bit scared, if you want to know. I asked Dad what was happening and he said it was God talking through the woman's mouth. Sending a message.'

Annabel nodded. 'I've heard of that. Speaking in tongues they call it only it's not, because when Jesus's disciples did it they used foreign languages they'd never learned, not gobbledegook.'

She frowned. 'What's he like, this Pastor Ken?'

Sarah shrugged under the duvet. 'He shouts and waves his arms about when he's preaching, but he's okay the rest of the time. He came and talked to Dad at the end.'

'Did he say anything to you?'

'No. He asked Dad who I was, then put his hand on my head and smiled. His real name's Mr Caster – I read it on a board.'

'Pastor Caster?' hooted Annabel. 'Sounds like an Italian starter.'

Sarah giggled again. 'Don't let Dad hear you say that.'

Annabel stood up. 'I don't care whether he hears me or not.' She looked down at her sister. 'D'you think you'll go again?'

Sarah pulled a face. 'I dunno. I might if Dad asks me. It was a bit boring, though.'

'I bet,' Annabel crossed to the door. 'Say no,' she whispered. 'I would.'

Sarah nodded. 'We'll see. Night, Annabel.'

'Night, kiddo. Sleep tight.'

Twenty-Three

'Annabel.' Ms Channing intercepted her as she entered the room with Celia. 'I'm sorry, but for the next two weeks you're to spend Geography periods doing individual study in the library. There's been a phone call from your father.'

Annabel gaped. 'A phone call? I don't — What sort of phone call, Miss?'

'Your father telephoned Mr Hately and asked that you be withdrawn from my lessons while we're dealing with the history of the Earth.'

'But he never said anything to *me*, Miss. It's *him* that's stopped believing in evolution, not me.' She saw Celia roll her eyes and felt her cheeks burn. Kids were nudging one another. Earwigging. 'Do I *have* to, Miss?'

The teacher nodded. 'The school is obliged to comply with your parent's request, Annabel.' She looked at her. 'Of course you can always read somebody's notes afterwards, but I'm not permitted to suggest that.'

'No, Miss.'

Apart from Mr Pugsley she had the library to herself. The librarian smiled and nodded as she passed his desk. He'd obviously been told to expect her. She chose a study table at which she'd be hidden from him by a fixture, and sat down.

Dad. She clenched her fists on the table. What a rotten thing to pull. Phoning like that, making me look a complete wally in front of the kids. You could have warned me. Better still, you could mind your own flipping business and let me mind mine.

Breathing deeply to calm herself, she glanced about her. Individual study. Nobody standing over her. No instructions as to *what* she should study. The choice was hers. Okay, then. She smiled thinly. The history of the Earth.

There were plenty of books on the subject, including the one Ten A were working from. She carried a copy of this to her table and leafed through it till she found what she was looking for. 600,000,000 years ago – earliest fossil evidence of invertebrates. That's what her classmates would be covering right now.

So, she told herself, if I read this section and the next and take notes I should be all right. What *is* the next section, anyway? She turned a few pages. Jawless fishes. She took her pencil and wrote in the margin, *Placed in the sea by Satan to lead mankind into error.* She looked at it and added, (*See section four thousand and nine for fossil evidence of Satan*). Then she turned back to the first invertebrates and began to read.

Twenty-Four

Break-time. Annabel walked out into the yard and was immediately accosted by Tim, Celia and Rodney. 'You missed a good 'un,' grinned Rodney. 'Old Channing stood on the table and did a strip.'

Annabel nodded. 'I believe you, Rodney, and I'm glad I wasn't there. Did you look at invertebrates as well?'

'Yeah. Riveting, it was. What did *you* do?'

'Same as you. I had a squint at jawless fishes too.'

'That's Wednesday,' said Tim.

Annabel nodded. 'I know. You crack on faster when you're by yourself.'

'Good on you, Annabel,' grinned Celia. 'You're certainly no Madeline Bray.'

'Eh?' went Rodney.

Celia smiled. 'Skip it, Rodney. You won't have got to that bit yet.'

'What's up with your dad, anyway?' asked Tim. 'Why can't you do the history of the Earth?'

Annabel sighed. 'It's that sect I mentioned to Mr Bickford on Friday, Tim. The Little Children. They don't believe in evolution.'

'So the history of the Earth starts with Adam and Eve?'

'As far as they're concerned, yes.'

'Crazy. I hope you're not going to end up wandering about in ankle socks, Annabel.'

She looked at him. 'Why ankle socks?'

He grinned. 'Haven't you noticed? Mad women *always* wear ankle socks. It's a sort of uniform.'

'Thanks a lot.' She smiled, keeping it light, but she was hurting inside. Her father's action had created a rift between her friends and herself. A rift which might easily widen.

They were drifting towards the field when a year eight kid approached them. 'Annabel Henshaw?'

'That's me.'

'Mr Hateley wants to see you in his office straight away.'

'Okay. Thanks.' She acted cool though her brain was yammering. What now? What the heck *now*, for pete's sake? The kid walked away. The others were watching her. She grinned. 'See you later, okay?' She turned and crossed the yard, feeling their eyes on her. She wanted to look back but was afraid that if she did she'd catch them whispering.

Twenty-Five

Her mother was having one of her good days and the meal was in course of preparation when Annabel got home. Sarah had set the table so there was nothing left for her to do. It was nice not to have to start cooking, but she could have done with something to keep her busy till Dad came in. She meant to challenge him but wasn't looking forward to it. To take her mind off the inevitable confrontation she went to her room and tried to read *Nicholas Nickleby*, but she couldn't concentrate.

At ten to six she heard the Renault and went down. When the family was seated and the usual banter was being exchanged she looked at her father and said, 'I wish you'd told me you were going to phone school, Dad.'

He paused with his fork half-way to his mouth. Annabel thought his cheeks flushed a bit but she might have imagined it.

Her mother looked at him. 'You phoned the school, dear? What about?'

Malcolm lowered his fork. 'It was nothing, Suzanne. Nothing to worry about. I was concerned about one or two items on the curriculum, that's all. I sorted it out with Mr Hateley. It's all right now.'

Annabel shook her head. 'No, it isn't, Dad. It isn't all right. For a start, the first I knew of it was when old Channing sprung it on me in front of all my friends. They were sniggering. I felt a total wimp. I had to work by myself in the library, and then at break-time the Head told me you wanted me out of R.E. as well – not just for a week or two, but permanently. R.E.'s one of my strong subjects, Dad – I'd have passed it easily. Now I can't take it at all, and it turns out you haven't even discussed it with *Mum*.'

Suzanne glanced from Malcolm to Annabel and back again. 'Let me get this straight,' she murmured. 'You've had Annabel withdrawn from some of her classes, dear. Is that it?'

Her husband nodded. 'That's correct.'

'But why? And why didn't you mention it to me? It's a very serious step, Malcolm. Annabel's future.'

'It's Annabel's future I'm *concerned* about, Suzanne. I won't have her head filled up with superstitions and half-baked theories.' He stabbed his cutlet and sawed at it with his knife. 'Evolution. Hinduism. What use are *they* in the real world?'

His wife shook her head. 'They're parts of a rounded education, Malcolm. You might as well ask what use is music or painting or dance. They might not get you a job, but the world would be a joyless place without them.'

'What about cross-country running?' asked Sarah. She disliked rows, and a row was brewing. She could feel it. The other three looked at her. 'What about it, dear?' inquired her mother.

'I hate it. The world would be a joyful place without it. Can you get me out of it, Dad?'

Suzanne shot her husband an amused look. 'Well, Malcolm – what about that? The use of cross-country running in the real world.'

She knew what Sarah was trying to do, but her husband refused to be drawn. 'This isn't funny, Suzanne. It's not a joke. I'm talking about wrong living here. Wrong living, and our need – our *desperate* need – to eliminate it.'

'*Your* desperate need, Dad,' said Annabel. 'Not ours. We were all okay till you discovered this nutty sect of yours.' She snorted. 'Three months Dad, that's all it's been, and you think you have the right to start messing about with *my* life.' She was crying now but rage propelled her and she laid into him, choking on the words. 'Who is this rotten Pastor anyway – Jesus Christ? The second coming? Is that who he *thinks* he is? What right does *he* have to say what I do at school?' She pushed back her chair and stood up, her food untasted. 'Pastor flipping Caster,' she yelled. 'The guy who put the *mental* in fundamentalism.' The chair went over backwards as she turned, blind with tears, and stumbled from the room.

Twenty-Six

'Longstaff?'

'Sir?'

'Cast what passes for your mind back one week, please.'

'Sir?'

'Tell us what we talked about.'

'Character assassination, sir.'

'I hope this is not an attempt at humour, laddie.'

'No, sir. It was character something, sir. I've forgotten the rest.'

'It was *characterisation*, you sad pleb. What was it?'

'Characterisation, sir.'

'Well?'

'Sir?'

'*Proceed*, Longstaff. Enlighten us all. Expound on the subject of characterisation.'

'Well, sir – er – there's two sorts of characters – round and flat, and this guy Chesterton reckoned . . .'

'Guy?' Mr Cordingley's neck swelled and reddened. 'G. K. Chesterton is not a *guy*, you ignoramus. G. K. Chesterton is a literary giant. I suppose you'll be referring to George Eliot as a *bird* next.' He sighed. 'Go on.'

Annabel gazed at her hands on the desk. Normally she'd have relished Old Rod's set-to with his hapless namesake, but not today. Today her body was in the classroom but her mind was not. Weren't things bad enough before, she asked herself, without all this Little Children stuff? Wasn't there enough to worry about? Mum ill. Dying, most likely. Nine hundred and thirty-four pages of *Nicholas Nickleby*. Exams next spring. *Crucial* exams. And now I'm a joke in school, thanks to Dad. No Geography. No R.E. What next? No P.E. because the kit shows my legs? No Shakespeare in case he mentions witches?

Tim. Tim already thinks I'm mad. Ankle socks. Will he still go out with me? I'll *die* if he won't, he's so brilliant. Oh, please don't let him pack me in. *Please, please, pleeeease* . . .

'Henshaw?' Annabel jumped. Old Rod was talking to her.

'S–sir?'

'Have you been *listening*, girl?'

'Yessir.'

'Good. Then you'll have no difficulty in explaining what we mean when we speak of a character as being flat.'

'Sir, it means . . . it means nothing affects them. Things go on all round them but they don't change. They're the same at the end as they were at the start.' And maybe that's the way to be, she thought. Flat.

I wish.

Twenty-Seven

'Suffer the little children to come unto me,' intoned the Pastor, 'for of such is the Kingdom of Heaven.' He smiled around the circle till his eyes came to rest on Malcolm. 'Perhaps you'd stay a moment, Brother.' The others were getting up with murmurs of halleluia and praise the Lord, going for their coats. Pastor Ken stood, acknowledging their good-nights with a smile and a nod as one by one they departed. Malcolm remained seated. When they were alone, the Pastor carried a chair across and sat down facing him.

'I sense you are troubled,' he said, without preamble. 'Sometimes it helps to talk.'

Malcolm, hands clasped between his knees, gazed at the floor. A part of him had wanted this opportunity, but now that he had it he found it difficult to begin. 'I – my wife.' He glanced up at the Pastor, then back at the dusty boards. 'Suzanne. She doesn't seem to be getting any better.'

Pastor Ken nodded. 'I'm so sorry, Malcolm. You know, don't you, that Suzanne is in all of our prayers?'

Malcolm nodded. 'I know, and I thought ... well, I hoped it would make a difference. You know – they talk about the power of prayer, don't they? I thought, with all the Brothers and Sisters praying for her, she'd improve.'

'And what do the doctors say about – ah – her prospects?'

Malcolm shook his head again. His throat constricted and his eyes filled with tears. He daren't look up and had to swallow before he could speak. 'It's not good, Pastor. She had radiotherapy but it didn't work. There are other things they can try, but I'm not . . . not . . .' Unable to hold it in any longer he hunched forward with his face in his hands and sobbed, feeling the Pastor's hand on his shoulder. It was several minutes before he regained sufficient control to pull out his handkerchief and mop his cheeks. 'I'm sorry. It's just that I keep trying to imagine life without her and I can't.' Pastor Ken squeezed his shoulder.

'I know, Brother. Things must look very black to you just now, but you mustn't despair. Miracles *do* happen. You've seen one or two yourself, in this very hall, and *I've* witnessed hundreds. I've seen the lame walk, the blind see . . . I've known hopeless cases – despaired of by the medical profession – recover completely through the elimination of wrong living. The laying on of hands. Through *faith*.'

'But – but they have to *be* here? For it to work I mean?'

'By no means. We've often prayed for bed-ridden relatives or friends and there's been complete recovery.' He smiled. 'After all, Jesus healed the Centurion's servant without seeing him.'

'So you think . . .?' Malcolm straightened up and pushed the crumpled handkerchief into his pocket. 'Suzanne?

The Pastor gave his shoulder another squeeze. 'Ah, well, you *see* Malcolm, Suzanne's case is . . . special.'

'Special?'

'Oh, yes.' He nodded gravely. 'You think because Suzanne shows no improvement *physically*, our prayers aren't working, but you see we're not praying for Suzanne's *body*. No. We're praying for her immortal *soul* because Suzanne isn't *saved*, and the pain she's suffering now is *nothing* compared to the torment she'll endure through all eternity if she doesn't come to the Truth.'

'You mean . . . you're all praying for her to *join* The Little Children?'

'Of course.'

'But she . . . there's *no* chance, Pastor. None at all. I thought we were praying for . . .'

'There's *always* a chance with Jesus, Malcolm. He seeks diligently the sheep that is lost.' He stood up. 'And now we must both be about our Father's business. God bless you, Brother.'

Twenty-Eight

Individual flipping study in the flipping library. Better be careful this time too – people about. Don't want some snitch reporting me for reading blasphemous material. Let's see – where was I? Invertebrates. Jawless fishes. Ah – this is it. First land plants. Funny – no mention of the tree of knowledge of good and evil. Ah, well . . .

Annabel read for a bit and scribbled some notes, but she couldn't concentrate. Partly it was people passing to and fro, but mostly it was anger. Why, she kept asking herself. Why should I have to sit here hiding my book just because Dad's let some weirdo get to him? What's this Pastor to do with *me*? I wouldn't be seen dead in his rotten church. It's not *fair*. What's Dad getting out of it, that's what I'd like to know.

She needed to talk to somebody about it, but who? Not the teachers. They had to do what Dad said. And not Tim or Celia. They thought the whole thing was a joke. Mum? No. She'd enough to worry about already.

Grandma. She could go see Grandma. *She'd* listen. She always did. You'd think old people would be preoccupied with their approaching deaths, but

Grandma always seemed to have time. Time to listen. She never looked at her watch.

The old lady lived in a bungalow on a senior citizen development. Annabel got there just after four. She thumbed the bellpush and waited. After a while she heard shuffling footsteps and the door opened on its chain.

'Annabel, what a lovely surprise.' The pale eyes searched her features. 'Is something the matter, dear?'

Annabel pulled a face. 'Bit of bother at home, Grandma. Can I talk to you?'

'Of course you may, Annabel.' She slipped the chain. 'Come on in. Let me take that jacket.'

Ten minutes later, sitting in an armchair with a mug of tea and a plate of chocolate biscuits, she'd told her story. 'I don't understand, Grandma,' she said. 'I don't know why Dad's got involved – what the attraction is. What is he getting out of it, that's worth messing up my school life?' She sat gazing at the artificial coals of the gas fire while the old lady digested what she'd been told. Grandma never responded hastily but when they came, her words were usually helpful and comforting. Presently she put her mug on a side table, folded her hands in her lap and began to speak.

'When your father was a little boy, we lived on the same street as a family of rag-and-bone men. Mawson, their name was. They had a field at the end of the street where they kept their carts and ponies. It was funny, because they'd built a bit of a shed for the carts but there was no shelter of any sort for the ponies. It was as if the Mawsons believed carts had feelings and ponies didn't.' The old lady smiled, remembering. 'Your dad loved those ponies. He was forever hanging over the fence, talking to them, offering handfuls of grass like kiddies do. Anyway, one night when he was eight we were coming home late from a Christmas party. It was a cold, windy night. There was a full moon and there were the ponies, standing in that patient way they have with their hindquarters to the wind and their manes and tails blown all one way, and he says, "Why don't they go in the shed, Mum?" "The shed's not for them," I told him. "It's full of carts." Well – you should have heard the commotion. He burst into tears. He was all for going to them, though what he·thought he could do I don't know. I had to drag him along the street. "It's not fair, Mum," he kept shouting. I had the devil's own job getting him to bed, and when I tucked him up he buried his face in the pillow and sobbed as if his heart would break.'

Grandma picked up her mug and sipped the tea. Annabel murmured, 'I can't imagine Dad like that.' After a moment the old lady set down the mug and continued.

'So there he was, breaking his heart, and suddenly an idea came to me. He used to say his prayers every night. A kid's prayer, you know – God bless Mummy and Daddy and so on. So I said, if you mention the ponies in your prayers, maybe God will keep them snug and warm till morning. "Will He really?" asked your dad.' Grandma smiled. 'You should have seen his little face.

'"I expect so," I told him. "He can do anything, you know." So from that night on your dad tagged the ponies on the end of his prayer and there were no more tears.'

Annabel waited, staring at the coals, but Grandma sipped her tea and said no more. Annabel thought about the old lady's story. After a while she looked across at her. 'So Dad stopped worrying but the ponies were still in the field?'

Grandma nodded. 'Yes. He'd left it with God, you see.' She sighed. 'Your dad's never been what you'd call a strong man, Annabel. Inside, I mean. When things have gone wrong he's tended to rely on others – your mum mainly – but now she's ill and he's finding her illness hard to accept. I suspect this . . . *sect* he's latched on to is a crutch – something to lean on so he won't feel alone. He may even believe they can *save* her.'

'Do *you* think they can, Grandma?'

The old lady shook her head. 'The ponies were still in the field, my dear,' she murmured.

Twenty-Nine

Malcolm Henshaw put the Renault keys in his pocket and yawned. It had been a hectic day. He pulled down the garage door and went into the house. Both his daughters were busy in the kitchen.

'Hello, you two. How's Mum?'

Annabel looked up from the carrots she was dicing. 'She's tired. D'you fancy swede with your carrots?'

He shrugged. 'Whatever.' He went through to the hallway to deposit his briefcase, then came back, frowning. 'Running a bit late, aren't we?'

'How d'you mean?' asked Annabel, scraping a mound of cubes into a pan with the back of the knife. Her father glanced at the kitchen clock. 'Five past six and you're just chopping the vegetables. Dinner's usually ready by this time.'

'I was a bit late in, Dad. I went to see Grandma straight after school.'

'Oh? Any particular reason?'

'Just to talk.'

'Hmmm. Well – quick as you like now, girls. Your father's starving.' He left the kitchen.

'What did you and Grandma talk about?' asked Sarah. She'd finished peeling the potatoes and was halving them.

'Oh, this and that,' said Annabel. 'Dad getting religion, mostly.'

'What does Grandma think about it?'

Annabel shrugged. 'She reckons he's doing it because Mum's ill. You know – looking for sympathy. Support. A miracle cure, maybe.'

The younger girl swallowed. 'Is that what it'll take, Annabel – a miracle?'

'What? Oh no, I didn't mean *that*, Sarah. I just meant he's unhappy because it's taking so long.' She cursed herself for her careless lapse. Sarah needn't know. Not just yet.

It was after seven when they dished up the meal. Mum didn't feel like coming to the table so Sarah carried a tray through with her mother's meal and her own. Annabel served her father and sat down facing him, sprinkling mint sauce on her lamb cutlet. He bent his head over his plate and she realised with surprise that he must be saying grace. She replaced the sauce boat quietly, feeling awkward. Then he looked up and said, 'We're robbing you of your childhood, Annabel.'

'What?' She thought he meant the cooking and cleaning. 'It's okay,' she said. 'I don't mind, honestly.'

His puzzled glance gave way to one of amusement. He shook his head. 'I don't mean *that*, Annabel. I'm talking about boy-friends. Lipstick. Scent. I mean late nights and lewd music. You're growing up too soon.'

'I'm fifteen, Dad,' she blurted, sensing danger.

'I'm not a child. *All* the girls have boy-friends and make-up.'

He nodded mildly. 'I know they do, Annabel, and it's wrong. Wrong living. Childhood is a blessed state of innocence. It should be prolonged, not curtailed at the earliest possible moment as it is today. I want you to stop seeing this – what's his name? Tim, isn't it?'

'Yes, it's Tim, and I won't stop seeing him, Dad. I *won't*. You can't make me.'

'I think you'll find I can, Annabel, but I hope it won't come to that. I hope to convince you it's the right thing for you to do.'

She shook her head, biting her lip to keep from crying. 'Never. I'll never give him up. He's the most brilliant boy I've ever met. If you interfere between me and him I'll run away.'

'Rubbish!' He looked up, chewing. 'Where would you go, Annabel? How would you live?' He snorted. 'You're just a couple of kids. When I was your age I didn't give a hoot about girls. Aeroplanes were my thing – a healthy, harmless hobby, which is what you should have instead of gallivanting round Salvo's with paint all over your face. Anyway.' He swallowed and attacked his cutlet again. 'I fancy the lad'll chuck you soon enough when you can't go out at night.'

Thirty

'Ah, Malcolm!' The Pastor greeted them at the door. 'And little Sarah, too.' He beamed at Sarah, who managed a smile though she resented his calling her little. The Pastor turned to greet another arrival and the two Henshaws moved on through the lobby.

There were about a dozen people in the big room. They stood in twos and threes, talking softly. In a far corner, two children were looking at a poster on the wall. One was the boy Malcolm had spoken with the week before. The other was a girl of about ten. Malcolm nodded towards them. 'Go say hello, sweetheart. I don't think either of them will be attending class. Keep one another amused and it'll be nine before you know it.'

She didn't want to. Both kids were younger than her – the boy couldn't be more than eight – but the adults were drifting towards the small room and she certainly didn't want to join them. Her father smiled encouragement. 'Go on, sweetheart – they won't bite.'

The poster showed a blond, blue-eyed Jesus sitting on something you couldn't see because of His voluminous white robes. He was surrounded by well-scrubbed children of various races and was smiling at them, while in the background two men in Arab dress looked on in obvious disapproval. As Sarah approached, the boy turned.

'Hello. I know who you are.'

'Do you?' asked Sarah.

'Yes. You're Brother Malcolm's daughter. Are you saved too?'

'What?'

'Are you saved, like your dad? Have you let Jesus into *your* life?'

'Oh, I dunno about that. I came because Dad asked me to. I didn't know he was – saved.'

'Well, he is. He's our brother, and soon you'll be our sister. I'm Andrew by the way, and this is Fiona. We've been saved a long time.'

'Uh – fine. I'm Sarah. I go to St Stephen's Primary but I'm moving up next summer. The Comp.'

The girl nodded. 'We're at Leyford Juniors. In different classes. We were looking at the picture. What do you think of it?'

Sarah gazed at the poster. What was she supposed to say? They were looking at her. 'It's colourful,' she murmured.

'Yes,' said Andrew, 'but look at His face. His eyes. Can't you see the love in them? He loves the little children.' He smiled at Sarah. 'That's why we call ourselves The Little Children, you know.'

Sarah nodded. 'I know.' She could have said a couple of things about the poster. That Jesus looked too English for a native of Palestine. Too spotless for a wandering teacher in a hot and dusty land, but she didn't. When you're the new kid it's best to keep your opinions to yourself.

Fiona looked around. 'They've gone in,' she said. 'What shall we do?'

The big hall was empty, the door to the side room closed. Andrew grinned. 'What about a game of footy?'

Fiona shook her head. 'Too noisy. Pastor Ken says it's all right to play, providing we don't make a noise. Football's *always* noisy.'

'If there's a ball,' said Sarah, 'we could play throw and catch. *That*'s not noisy.' It was obvious from Andrew's expression that throw and catch wasn't *his* favourite thing, but Fiona backed Sarah's suggestion and so they formed the points of a triangle and lobbed the plastic soccer ball to one another till they tired of it. Then they unfolded three stacking chairs and sat down. It was twenty past eight. A drone of voices sounded through the side room door. Forty minutes to go.

'You off to Faith Camp?' asked Andrew, addressing Fiona. The girl nodded. 'Can't wait. The stream. Those autumn colours. It was brilliant last year.'

The boy pulled a face. 'I couldn't go last year. Too young. I was at the spring one, though.' He grinned. 'I fell off that bridge we built. Got soaked.'

'I remember. Brother Neil pulled you out, gave you a piggy-back up to the Brothers' tent.'

'Yeah.' Andrew smiled. 'He rubbed me down

with this really scratchy towel and I had to walk about with it wrapped round me till my clothes were dry. I looked such a wally he took my picture.' The pair chuckled, remembering.

'What's Faith Camp?' asked Sarah. Fiona smiled.

'You'll find out. We have 'em three times a year, at a place called Eden Vale. It's brilliant. All the kids go, and Pastor Ken and some of the grown-ups. We do all sorts. Midnight hikes. Building bridges. Singing round the camp fire. It's next month, at half-term. Will your dad let you come?'

Sarah shrugged. 'I dunno. I could ask him.'

'Ask, then. You'll love it, honestly. Won't she, Andrew?'

'Oh, yeah.' He grinned. 'Specially midnight hikes.'

Andrew and Fiona reminisced about camps they'd attended. Sarah wasn't at all sure she wanted to go next month – she wouldn't know anybody and certainly wasn't saved, but she listened, interposing a question now and then, till the scrape of chairs in the side room signalled the end of the class.

Riding home in the Renault she answered her father's questions about the two children, whom he referred to as her new friends, but she didn't mention camps. She'd talk to Mum about it first, or maybe Annabel. If they thought it sounded okay, and if she decided to continue going to meetings, then perhaps she'd mention it to Dad. It was six weeks away after all.

Thirty-One

Annabel was heading for her room when Sarah called her name. She went in and sat on her sister's bed and Sarah told her what had happened at the Citadel.

'Faith Camp?' Annabel pulled a face. 'Sounds pretty gruesome to me, kiddo. Cold plunges, burnt porridge and hymns round the camp fire. I'd forget it if I were you.'

'Andrew and Fiona said it was brilliant.'

'Yeah, well – they're probably brainwashed.'

'How d'you mean?'

'They brainwash you, religious sects. They've brainwashed Dad, Sarah. He doesn't believe in dinosaurs, but he *used* to. He thinks fifteen's too young for boy-friends, but he never did before. Haven't you noticed how he's *changing*?'

Sarah nodded. 'He's different, but I thought it was because of Mum. He's happy at the Citadel, though, you can tell.'

'And you – what do *you* think of the Citadel?'

Sarah shrugged. 'It's okay. Bit boring hanging about, and that Andrew's weird. He talks like a grown-up.' She grinned. '"Have you let Jesus into *your* life," he says, and he's eight, at the most.'

'There you are,' nodded Annabel. 'Brainwashed.'

'So what do you think I should do?'

Annabel shook her head. 'I dunno, kiddo. I think they're sinister, people like them. Dangerous. If it was me I'd stay well clear, but I can't decide for you.' She smiled. 'Why don't you talk to Mum about it? I'm a bit biased because of the way Dad's messing with my life, but Mum'll help you decide. Besides.' She sighed. 'You might have to get used to not having me to talk to.'

'Why?' Sarah's eyes widened. 'You're not . . .'

'Sssh!' Annabel pressed a finger to her lips. 'Yes, I'm thinking of going away if Dad doesn't stop interfering.' She snorted. 'He told me last night I should have a hobby. A *hobby*. Can't you just see it? Me, sticking flipping stamps in an album or watching bluetits through binoculars. The excitement'd kill me in a week.'

Sarah giggled, then shook her head. 'Don't go, Annabel. I don't want you to. Things'll get better, you'll see. I know!' She grabbed a handful of her sister's sleeve. 'I could talk to Dad. Tell him how fed up you are. He'll listen to me, I *know* he will.'

'No!' Annabel gripped the child's thin shoulder. 'You mustn't say a word, Sarah. Not a word. I might not go – I haven't decided yet, but if I *do* I don't want him warned beforehand.' She relaxed her grip and gazed into Sarah's eyes. 'It's a secret, kiddo. *Our* secret. I'm trusting you. Okay?'

'Okay, only . . .'

'What?'

'Wait till Mum's better, Annabel. Don't go while she's ill. Promise?'

'I . . .' Annabel stood up. 'Don't worry, kiddo. Sleep tight. See you tomorrow.'

Thirty-Two

I'm usually available at break-times and after school, Baldy Bickford had said. At break-time Friday morning Annabel knocked on the staff-room door. Old Rod opened it. 'Yes, Henshaw?'

'Is B . . . is Mr Bickford in, sir?'

'I believe so.'

'Can I speak to him please, sir?'

'You *can*, of course. Whether or not you *may* is another matter. Wait there.'

She waited. After a moment Mr Bickford appeared. 'What can I do for you, Annabel?'

'Sir, Ten A's got you after break, but I'm withdrawn. I wondered if you'd tell me what you'll be doing so I can read it up in the library?'

'Hmmm.' The teacher frowned. 'I think we'd best discuss this in my room, Annabel.' He closed the staff-room door. 'Come along.'

Seated in the class-room, he looked at her. 'I know what you're trying to do, Annabel, and I sympathise. R.E.'s one of your strong subjects and you'd probably walk the exam, but I'm afraid it won't work.' He picked up a ball-point and fiddled with it, trying to balance it on its tip. 'A lot of my sessions are done through discussion. There's not a lot of reading, and of course you can't do the discussion bits by yourself.' He clicked open the ball-point, then retracted it. 'You could talk to your friends after each session, I suppose – ask them what we covered – but it wouldn't be all that effective and, anyway, I can't enter you for the exam – not when your father's withdrawn you.'

Annabel stared at her hands on the scarred table. 'My dad – I think he thinks The Little Children can make Mum better. She's got cancer, you see.'

'Oh, Annabel . . . I'd no idea. How dreadful.' He clicked the ball-point in and out. 'Your doctor – what does he think?'

'She,' corrected Annabel tonelessly. 'I don't know, really. They don't tell me much but I think it's pretty bad.' She looked up, swallowing the lump in her throat. 'Do *you* believe in faith-healing, sir?'

He shook his head. 'I don't know, Annabel, but . . . well, I don't think you should – you know – entertain false hope. There have been instances – countless instances – of seemingly miraculous cures, or at least remissions, but there have been countless failures, too, and nobody has ever explained why it works in some cases and not in others.'

'So you think Dad's kidding himself?'

The teacher pulled a face. 'I might not want to put it *quite* like that, Annabel. I suspect he's clinging desperately on to anything he can find that seems to offer hope, which is probably what *I'd* do in his place, but fundamentalism . . .' He sighed, put down the pen and sat back in his chair. 'Do you know what a panacea is, Annabel?'

Annabel nodded. 'It's something that cures everything, isn't it, sir?'

'That's right, and of course it doesn't exist. Fundamentalists of every sort – religious and political – have one thing in common. They believe that *their* system, whatever it is, is the panacea the world's been waiting for. Embrace *our* philosophy, they say – follow *our* programme – and everything will be fine. No more suffering. No more injustice. Join us, and you can stop worrying about the world.'

Annabel nodded. 'And that's what The Little Children are – fundamentalists?'

The teacher nodded. 'Sounds like it to me, Annabel. The rejection of evolutionary theory is common among Christian fundamentalists. They're extremists, and like all extremists they insist their members close their minds to any sort of moderating influence.'

'I'm not sure I know what you mean, sir.'

'Well, let's take evolution as an example. Most Christian thinkers today accept that there *is* such a thing as evolution – that creatures change in order to adapt to changing conditions, and that those creatures which can't change, or fail to change quickly enough, die out. And because they accept this, they recognise the story of Adam and Eve for what it is – a creation myth. But that doesn't cause them to lose their faith. No. They say okay – so the world *wasn't* made in six days, but it's still a wonderful world and it didn't come about by accident. *God* made it – dinosaurs, cavemen and all. The fact that it's taken millions of years and that it's *still* changing doesn't make it any less miraculous. If anything it *adds* to the wonder, but fundamentalists don't see this. According to them, it's necessary to believe in the literal truth of every word in the Bible, even where the advance of knowledge has shown it to be inaccurate.'

'Hmmm.' Annabel stared at her clasped hands. 'So there's nothing I can do about R.E., sir?'

Mr Bickford shook his head. 'I'm afraid not, Annabel. The school is required by law to respect your parent's wishes, but . . .'

'But what, sir?'

The teacher smiled wryly. 'I was going to say the law doesn't require you to become a fundamentalist, Annabel, but I mustn't, so I won't.' He stood up. 'You know you can come and see me any time, don't you? If you want to talk, I mean?'

Annabel rose. 'Yes, sir. Thank you, sir.' She looked at him.

'Two things I'll never be. Madeline Bray and a fundamentalist. 'Bye, sir.'

'Goodbye, Annabel.' He watched with a bemused frown as his pupil left the room.

Thirty-Three

Lunch-time, Tim was waiting on the step. 'Where were you at break, Annabel? We were looking all over for you.'

'I had to see Baldy. What did you want me for?'

'Millennium're opening that new music place at the Mall tomorrow morning. Eleven o'clock.'

'What – all four of 'em?' Millennium was Annabel's favourite band.

'Of *course* all four. They're inseparable, aren't they? We're getting there early 'cause it's gonna be packed. Island, ten o'clock, okay?' Annabel nodded. 'If I can.'

'How d'you mean *if you can*? We're talking Millennium, Annabel. When they played Ireland, guys walked *eleven* miles out of Dublin and eleven back to be there. They were getting home at five in the morning.'

'I know, Tim, but it's Dad. You can never tell with him these days. I'll do my best.'

He snorted. 'You *be* there if you want to hang out with us. We don't need any couch potatoes holding *us* back.'

Over dinner that evening Annabel said, 'Millennium

are opening a music place at the Mall tomorrow. I'm meeting some of the others.'

Mum was having one of her good days. She smiled. 'That'll be exciting for you, dear. Your dad and I once saw The Swinging Bluejeans open a supermarket in Wolverhampton.' She looked at her husband. 'D'you remember, Malcolm? We'd only just met. It was one of our first outings as a couple.'

Malcolm nodded. 'You were twenty, Suzanne, not fifteen, and I was twenty-two.'

'Oh, but there were plenty of fifteen-year-olds *there*, darling,' She chuckled. 'I remember feeling positively middle-aged among all those teenagers.'

Her husband shook his head. 'Those were wicked times, Suzanne. We didn't realise it, but they were. Drugs. Permissiveness. Young men with shoulder-length hair, wearing mascara and dressing like girls.' He looked at his daughter. 'You're not to go, Annabel. You can concentrate on your homework for once, instead.'

Annabel was not totally surprised. She stared at the tablecloth as her mother attempted a mild intercession. 'Oh, but Malcolm – aren't you being a bit hard? After all . . .'

'I'm being hard for her own *good*, Suzanne. For *all* our good. There's too much *slackness* about parenting these days. It's a major cause of wrong living.'

Annabel could have started a row. The anger was certainly there, but he was no doubt expecting it and it wouldn't sway him. There was a better way, arising out of her talks with Grandma and with

Baldy. She gazed at him and spoke quietly. 'It won't work, you know, Dad. The Little Children are just a bunch of plonkers looking for a panacea, and there *is* no panacea.' She stood up. 'You can jump through hoops for Pastor Caster till you're blue in the face but the ponies'll still be in the field.' And I'll be at the Mall tomorrow, too, she thought but didn't say. In the silence which followed, she turned and left the room.

Thirty-Four

She set her alarm for seven. Nobody in the Henshaw household stirred before eight on Saturdays. She'd skip breakfast and be away before anyone knew.

As often happens with alarms, she woke before it beeped. By five past seven she was dressed and out of the house. God, five past seven. Nearly three hours before I meet the others. Four till the actual opening. What the heck shall I *do*?

It was a chill morning. Damp flags and beaded webs. A black cat crossed the road. Apart from herself it was the only sign of life in Linden Drive. Annabel decided to go down to the canal and stroll on the towpath. She'd always been attracted by water. Beneath its surface was a world whose inhabitants couldn't survive in air. It was almost like another planet – an alien environment into which humans ventured at their peril and yet it was once their element. Their home, which is why it exerted a fascination. Life began in water, and everyone has an underwater life before they learn to breathe.

There was mist on the dark water. Overhanging sycamores were beginning to lose their leaves which floated, freckling the black with yellow. There was nobody about. It was cold for strolling so Annabel walked briskly, and by eight o'clock she was in open country four miles from home. She'd seen a heron, a dead roach and an old man with a spaniel. A watery sun had dispersed the mist. If she turned round now and strolled back, it'd be time to call for Celia.

It was twenty-five past nine when she knocked on Celia's door. Mr Buckley opened it. 'Come in a minute, Annabel.' He grinned. 'She's making herself look nice for Keg so it could be hours yet.' Keg played drums with Millennium. Annabel liked Mig better. She wished her dad was like Celia's.

It wasn't hours, and Celia looked great. Annabel wished *she*'d been able to spend a bit of time on her hair instead of just dragging a brush through it, but she hadn't, and the eight-mile walk had probably made it worse.

'Eight *miles*?' cried Celia as the pair set off to walk into town. 'You must be barmy, Annabel. What time did you get up?'

'Sevenish.' She explained how she'd had to dodge her father. 'I expect he'll half kill me when I get home, but it's worth it.' She smiled dreamily. 'Mig.'

'They won't notice us,' sighed Celia. 'They won't even *see* us, there'll be so many there.'

'Didn't stop you tarting yourself up though, did it?' said Annabel. 'Wish *I* looked like you.'

'Oh, stop it, Annabel. You look *fine*.' She grinned. 'For somebody who's done an eight-mile hike.'

The Mall was busy already, but Tim and Rodney had bagged a table at Island. The girls got Cokes and joined them. 'Told you we'd better be early,' crowed Tim. 'If we'd waited till quarter to eleven we'd not have got near.' He peered at Annabel. 'Have you been out all night or what?'

'No, I haven't, you cheeky pig.' She repeated her explanation.

'Your dad's gone nuts, if you ask me,' said Tim when she'd finished. 'They want to put him in a rubber room and lose the key.'

'He's got a lot of stress,' said Annabel defensively, 'with Mum and all.' Dad wasn't her favourite person right now but Tim's words had nettled her. He'd no right to talk about her father that way.

Tim shrugged. 'Yeah, I know, but still . . .'

'Don't you think we'd better get in line?' interrupted Celia. 'People're *pouring* in.'

Rodney nodded. 'I think you're right.' He stood up. 'What I don't understand is why anybody wants to gawp at a bunch of uglies like Mig, Keg, Spud and Mowglie when there's me and Tim to look at.'

'They've come to see *men*, not monkeys,' snorted Celia. 'Come on.'

Thirty-Five

The concourse in front of the supermarket was thronged with fans and shoppers. The four friends would have seen very little if Rodney hadn't led the way grunting, 'Scuse me – let the lads *through* if you want to see 'em.' Everybody assumed he was a minder or a roadie and made a gangway which the four strode down like the Israelites crossing the Red Sea. By the time spectators realised they'd been had, it was too late.

Millennium were late too. Ten minutes late. And when they finally showed up they didn't come through the crowd. They emerged through one of the supermarket's glass and steel doors, ducking under the yellow tape they'd soon be cutting. Screams and cheers greeted the four musicians as they straightened up, grinning and waving. Mig was apologetic. 'Sorry to keep you guys hanging about – we got stuck behind a Lada.' The ripple of laughter evidently encouraged him, because his grin broadened and he said, 'Talking about Ladas – what's the difference between a Lada and a Jehovah's Witness?' He waited, scanning the crowd, but nobody knew. He shrugged. 'Easy – you can close the door on a Jehovah's Witness.'

As the crowd roared its appreciation, Annabel felt her right arm seized and a voice hissed, 'It's home for you my girl – right now!'

Glancing sharply sideways she saw her father's furious face and felt herself being dragged backwards. 'What're you *doing*?' She lashed out with her free hand, really trying to hurt him. 'Get off me, you nutter!'

A mixture of shock, fear and embarrassment scrambled her brain. They won't notice us, Celia had said, but as she tottered back from the rope which separated the band from the crowd, she saw Mig's startled glance and knew her hero had witnessed her ignominy. 'I'll *kill* you!' she screamed at her father, and meant it.

For the second time the spectators were making a gangway as the grim-faced man marched through, dragging his kicking, spitting daughter. She heard laughter and cheers, like when somebody drops a stack of plates at school dinners, and then Rodney's voice, loud and clear, cried. 'She's *fifteen*, you plonker, not five.' It was her last lucid moment as, blind with tears of rage and humiliation, she was hustled away.

Thirty-Six

Annabel lay motionless on her bed as afternoon became evening. She lay on her stomach with her face buried in the pillow, which was damp from her tears, but she'd stopped crying now. Surges of rage and shame possessed her as her mind played back, over and over, the video it had recorded. A lot of it was blurry but certain bits were all too sharp. Mig's startled glance. Rodney's voice. Her father's face. There was no pause button, no off. She pressed her face into the pillow and screwed up her eyes but she could still see it, and she could hear it even when she clamped her hands to her ears and shouted.

I can't stand it. I can't. He's made everything impossible. *Everything*. I can't go to school. Think what it'd be like. What they'd say. Especially Rodney. And it'll get out. The whole *school*'ll know. Kids'll snigger every time I show my face – even the little ones. There's Annabel, they'll say. Her dad's crazy, you know. Showed her up in front of half the town. Dragged her home just 'cause she wanted to see Mig McGee. Wonder if he smacked her bottom and sent her to bed? Bet he did.

Well, he didn't, so there. Smack me I mean. I'd have killed him if he had. But he *did* send me to bed, or anyway to my room, which amounts to the same thing. GO TO YOUR ROOM. Like something out of a Victorian melodrama. I DON'T WANT TO SEE YOUR FACE AGAIN TILL MONDAY MORNING. D'you think I want to see *yours*, you pathetic headcase? No way. Never again.

I'm out of here Monday. I *told* him I'd go and I will. He'll be sorry then, but it'll be too late. Where would you go, he says. London, Dad, that's where. You'll not find me there. You won't drag me home *this* time. I'll get a job. *Any* job. Supermarket. Coffee shop. And then I'll do whatever I like. I'll have my own dosh, see? *Nobody* can tell you what to do when you've got your own dosh.

Thirty-Seven

Sunday morning, half-past nine. A knock on Annabel's door. Sarah with a tray. Annabel's still in her nightie. Her hair's a mess and it's plain she's been crying.

'Breakfast,' says Sarah.

'Thanks.' Annabel takes the tray. 'Want to come in?'

'Dad says not to. What *happened*, Annabel?'

'I don't want to talk about it. You'd better go.'

'I don't like this, Annabel. It's funny downstairs without you.'

'It's not a million laughs up here, either, kiddo. You off to that place tonight?'

'The Citadel?'

'Yeah. Are you?'

'I think so. Dad's off this morning too, but Mum needs me here.'

'She needs *him* here, Sarah.'

'No. She'll get better quicker if he keeps going there. Pastor Ken promised.'

'I bet. Listen. Remember that trip from school? When you went to the Natural History Museum?'

'Yes.'

'Remember the best bit? The bit you went on and on about when you got back?'

'Standing in the dinosaur footprint, you mean?'

'Right. That was a *real* footprint, wasn't it? Left in mud millions of years ago by an actual dinosaur?'

'That's what the man said. The museum man.'

'Yes, and he should know 'cause he's the expert. So don't you let *anyone* tell you there never were any dinosaurs, Sarah. Not even Dad.'

'Why should Dad say that? *He* knows there were. He used to show me the pictures in that book I had when I was about six.'

'He doesn't believe in dinosaurs now, kiddo. Not since Pastor Caster got to work on his brain. You see they don't get to work on *yours*. Off you go now.'

Sarah leaves. Annabel closes the door, looks at her tray. Egg and bacon. Toast. A mug of tea. *He* cooked it. Must have. Mum's no good in the mornings. I'm not eating anything *he's* cooked. I'd rather starve. I'll drink the tea, though. Sarah probably made that.

Lot to do today. One good thing about being exiled up here – no-one's going to bother me. I'll pack my stuff in my school bag. Not school stuff – clothes and that. It'll look the same. I'll only take what I *really* need. I won't forget the dosh in my knicker drawer. Forty-five quid. Then there's my piggy-bank. Six or seven quid in there, I reckon.

What else? Toothbrush. Hairbrush. Lipstick. Comb. Not *Nicholas Nickleby*. That's *two* things I'll be glad to leave behind. *Nicholas Nickleby*, and Dad.

Not Mum, though. And not Sarah, poor kid. Wait till Mum gets better, she says, but I can't, kiddo. I *can't*. And anyway Mum's not *going* to get better. Grandma knows. The ponies were still in the field, she said.

Suppose ... no. If I start supposing I'll never leave. She'll be okay till I get back. It'll bring Dad to his senses, me leaving, then I can come home. It's just for a while. She'll be fine till then.

Why couldn't things just stay the way they were?

Thirty-Eight

She couldn't sleep for thinking. Mum. Sarah. Tim. Celia. There's more to leaving home than just packing a bag. Is it the right thing, especially with Mum as she is? Does it make sense, and have I any choice after what happened yesterday? Could I carry on as if it never happened? No. They wouldn't let me, and anyway who knows what Dad'll come up with next? How do I say goodbye to Mum in the morning, then? To Sarah? The way you do it *every* Monday morning, that's how, otherwise you'll give the game away. I don't know if I *can*.

She got up at half-past seven, feeling awful. Her eyes itched and her stomach churned. The word butterflies came into her mind, but these weren't butterflies in her tummy. More like hippos. She took her turn in the bathroom, thinking it's the last time. The *last* time. Where will I wash tomorrow? She couldn't make it feel real.

Breakfast seemed to drag on forever. The only good thing was that they put her silence and lack of appetite down to what had happened over the weekend. It was bad when Dad left, because he took Sarah with him. It was drizzling and his route took him close to her school. She might be seeing the kid for the last time and all she could do was smile wanly and murmur, 'See you tonight.'

Mum was worst, though. As the sound of the Renault faded she shook her head. 'I've lost him, you know, to that sect. He's not the same man, and they'll get Sarah too, you'll see. Once those people have their hooks in you they never let go.' She smiled sadly at Annabel. 'It's a good job there's you darling, or I'd be all alone.' Annabel's eyes filled with tears and she had to dash upstairs.

She almost changed her mind as she sat sobbing on the bed. It was only by switching on the video inside her head and watching a replay of Saturday's humiliation that she was able to stop crying, dry her eyes and go downstairs with her bag.

She managed to walk dry-eyed out of the house, but she sniffled as she hurried along Linden Drive with her head down. She stuck to her usual route till she knew she couldn't be seen from the house, then took a right down Sycamore Way and headed for the station, mopping her cheeks with a Kleenex. Mustn't look upset at the ticket booth.

'Single to London, please.'

'Standard?'

'What?'

'D'you want standard class?' The clerk sounded irritable.

'Oh, yes, please. What time's the next one?'

'It's on the monitor. They do *teach* reading at your school, I suppose?' Sarcastic little rat. Still, it kept her mind off other things.

She passed through the barrier and studied the monitor. 09.15. Platform 3. She put her bag down and looked at her watch. 08.44. Half an hour. Oh well, at least I'm out of the rain.

She went into the women's lavatory, stripped off her damp uniform and put on jeans and a jacket. Then she stuffed her blazer, blouse and skirt into her bag, splashed cold water on her face, mopped it with a tissue and brushed her hair before a mildewed mirror. The activity served to subdue the lump in her throat and kill fifteen minutes. She crossed the footbridge feeling much better and wishing she'd eaten breakfast.

There were quite a few people on platform 3. Annabel stood beside an iron pillar with her head down in case there was someone she knew, but there didn't seem to be.

There was a rush when the train pulled in, and the vacant seats were quickly taken. Annabel had to ask a man to remove his briefcase from the aisle seat next to his own. He dumped it on her bit of the table, and when she sat down he turned away and stared out of the window to show that he didn't intend shifting it. The two men opposite had newspapers up in front of them. She could see only their fingers and the tops of their heads. She sighed, sat back and closed her eyes. The train started to move.

Thirty-Nine

It was twenty past ten when the train pulled into Euston. The man next to Annabel was obviously in a hurry, because he stood up before they were anywhere near the platform. He didn't say excuse me, but stared stonily down at her till she moved, then jostled her as she stretched up to the rack for her bag. His shove and the braking of the train made her stagger sideways and she had to grab someone's shoulder to keep from falling. 'S-sorry,' she gasped, as the man who'd pushed her strode off down the train. ''S all right, duck. No harm done.' The shoulder's owner grinned up at her. Thank goodness there are *some* nice people about.

It was dry in London. The sun was out. Annabel turned left along Eversholt Street. It was a broad, busy street and she knew she wouldn't find a room on it. She crossed over and walked north. Ten A would be going into geography now. Old Channing'd assume she'd gone straight to the library till somebody – probably Celia – told her otherwise, then she'd think she was off sick. The kids wouldn't, though. *They'd* think she was wagging off because she couldn't face them after Saturday and they were right, but they'd no idea how far away she was or how long it'd be before they saw her again.

She walked on, reading street names. Polygon. Aldenham. Cranleigh. On a whim she turned into Cranleigh Street, walked the length of it and took a left on Chalton, where there was a parade of little shops under some flats. One was a post office with cards taped on its window. On the cards were adverts in biro or pencil. *R + A Baxter light haulage no item too small. FOR SALE Baxi Bermuda as new. No reasonable offer refused. BRITT. Swedish masseuse. Very rigorous. Room. Suit working man. Apply in person 144 Goldington Cresc.* Hmmm. Suit working man. Why not working woman? I'm *not* working, but I soon will be, won't I? Where's Goldington Crescent, I wonder? She went in and asked, and it turned out she'd have come to it if she'd walked on a bit further. Things were looking good.

It was a four-storey Victorian house in a run-down terrace. Its area railings were rusty, its door blistered. The stone sills under the windows had been painted orange, but not recently. Annabel mounted some greasy steps and rang the bell. Footfalls, a metallic scraping noise and the door opened to reveal a slim Asian youth with a thin moustache.
'Yeah?'

'I've come about the room.'

'Room?'

'Yes. I saw the ad in the post office.'

'Oh, the room. What about it?'

'I – I'd like to see it, please. I'm new in London and I need somewhere to stay.'

The youth smiled fleetingly and shook his head. 'Not here. You wouldn't want to stay here. It's a room for a man.'

'I don't mind, honestly. I'd like to see it.'

'Well . . .' He looked doubtful. 'My dad's out at the moment. I don't know what he'll say, but I suppose you can look.' He stepped aside. 'Come on in, but you won't like it.'

She followed him up two flights of stairs, the second of which was uncarpeted. There were cooking smells and the thin reek of damp. The thumping rhythm of a rock number reached the dim landing from somewhere. The young man stopped by a door, unlocked it and pushed it open. 'This is it. Not exactly Buckingham Palace, is it?'

Annabel walked in. An iron bedstead. Faded linoleum. A tiny washbasin under a geyser in a corner. A small table and two chairs against the wall where the ceiling sloped down. A sash window, uncurtained. She looked out and saw rooftops. She turned. The youth was leaning on the doorframe, hands in pockets. 'There doesn't seem to be . . . how do I cook?'

'Shared kitchen two doors down. Bathroom at the end, also shared. Two guys. One works nights. Fifty a week, month in advance.'

It was some seconds before she realised he meant the rent. She swallowed. 'Fifty *pounds*? A *week*?'

He nodded. 'That's the one. You got it?'

'I . . . no. Not yet. I can give you thirty now and the rest later. I'm getting a job, you see.'

He snorted. 'You got thirty quid and no *job*?' He straightened up. 'Come on, darling – let's have you out of here.'

'But I'll get a job. I don't care what it is. I'll get it today. And here . . .' She fumbled out her purse, opened it. 'Thirty pounds. It's all I've got. I'm very clean, very quiet . . .'

He jerked his head over his shoulder. 'Out.'

They descended. This time he followed her. In the hallway stood a middle-aged Pakistani woman. She spoke sharply to the youth, who muttered something and went through a door. The woman looked at Annabel. 'How old are you, please?'

Annabel sniffed, feeling for a tissue. 'Seventeen.'

'You come to London today – first time today?'

Annabel dabbed her eyes with the tissue. 'Yes.'

'Go home, child. No good here.'

She shook her head. 'I can't.'

'Can't?' The woman's eyes searched hers. 'You have a mother?'

Annabel nodded. She daren't speak or she'd burst into tears.

The woman nodded. 'That mother. She will cry for you. Go home.'

'I told you – I *can't*.' She moved towards the door she'd come in by. It was open. As she hurried down the steps the woman called after her. '*I* am a mother with children far away. I *know*.'

Forty

Suzanne Henshaw looked at her watch. Five o'clock. 'Sarah?'

Her younger daughter popped her head round the door. 'Yes, Mum?'

'You haven't seen Annabel, I suppose?'

'No, Mum. She's not in yet.'

'But it's five o'clock.'

'Maybe there's a rush on at Quicksave.'

'Monday teatime? It's not very likely, is it? I'm wondering whether I should call the school.'

Sarah shrugged. 'I'd wait a bit, Mum. She'll be here.'

At ten past Suzanne lifted the cordless phone and punched in the school number. Somebody picked up on the second ring. 'Meadway Comprehensive, Hateley speaking.'

'Oh, Mr Hateley, it's Suzanne Henshaw. Annabel's mother. I'm sorry to trouble you, but it's ten past five and my daughter's not home. I wondered whether she got a detention or something?'

'But Mrs Henshaw – Annabel hasn't been to school today. We assumed she was unwell.'

'Not been to school? I don't understand, Mr Hateley. Are you sure? She left home at the usual time.'

'I'm *absolutely* sure, Mrs Henshaw. I have the register in front of me.'

'Then where . . . I think I'd better phone the police. Thanks, Mr Hateley.' She cut him off, started to dial 999, then cancelled. Was it 999 for something like this? Did this count as an emergency? Suppose Annabel was just truanting?

Sarah looked in. 'Who were you talking to, Mum?'

'Mr Hateley. Annabel hasn't been to school today. D'you think she wagged off, darling? Did she say anything to you?'

Sarah shook her head. 'No, she didn't. Why don't you try Celia Buckley? She might know.'

Her mother nodded. 'Worth a try, I suppose.'

As she watched her mother punch Celia's number, Sarah remembered something her sister had said a few evenings ago. *You might have to get used to not having me to talk to.* As her mother spoke into the phone, she slipped out and went upstairs.

'. . . yes, I *know* she was very upset, Celia. Perhaps you're right. Perhaps she *couldn't* face her friends. I pray to God it hasn't made her . . . well, thank you, Celia. I hope so too. Yes, of course I'll let you know. Goodbye.'

'Mum?' Suzanne glanced up. Sarah looked pale. 'What is it, darling?'

'I – I looked in Annabel's room, Mum. Some of her clothes have gone, and all her money. I think she's run away.'

Forty-One

By midday she'd been ravenous, thinking about the kids trooping into dinners. Monday. Beef olives, probably, with a choice of baked potatoes or chips, and rhubarb crumble and custard for pudding. She'd spent one pound forty on a slice of pizza and a tea, leaving herself with twenty-eight pounds sixty. At two o'clock a guy sitting in a doorway had mumbled, 'Got any spare change?' and she'd given him twenty pence before it struck her that if she didn't find work in the next few hours she was going to be in the same boat herself.

Work. There *had* to be work in a place the size of London. Cafés. Kiosks. All these shops. A shoe shop would be nice, or a hairdresser's, but anything would do for a start.

There was nothing. She couldn't believe it. Sorry, love. Work? You're joking – we're letting two girls go, Saturday. Got experience, have you? No? Then I can't use you dear. Sorry. Her feet ached, she was hungry again and the sun had gone down behind the buildings.

Twenty-eight pounds forty. Surely I can get a bed *somewhere* for that? Less than that. The Y.W.C.A. The Sally Army. Trouble is I'm only fifteen so they'd send me home. I read that somewhere.

Dusk. They'll know now. Mum'll be frantic. I should've left a note, shouldn't I? *Don't worry, I can take care of myself.* Wouldn't be true, though, would it? Look at me. No job. No room. Hardly any dosh. Great start, right?

Not going back, though. No way. Not till Dad's over this Little Children thing. He'll be feeling bad already for driving me out. I *should've* put it in a note though, just to make sure. *Dad has made my life intolerable.* He's probably running to Pastor flipping Caster right now, hoping he can *pray* me home.

That'll be the day.

Forty-Two

'Mother? Malcolm.'

'Oh, hello dear. How's Suzanne?'

'Suzanne's fine. Is Annabel with you?'

'Annabel? No, dear. I haven't seen her since last Wednesday. Is something *wrong*, Malcolm?'

'She's disappeared, Mother. Taken clothes and money and gone off somewhere.'

'Oh, my God. Where have you tried? Janey's? Her friends?'

'We're *doing* it, Mother. I'm going to hang up now, try someone else.'

'The police, Malcolm. Phone the police. She's under age. They'll do something.'

'Yes, Mother, we've thought of that. I'll call them as soon as I've checked friends and relatives. I've got to go now.'

'She was very upset last Wednesday, Malcolm, about this religious sect you've got yourself into. I wouldn't be surprised if *that*'s what's made her run off.'

'Yes, thank you, Mother. We've thought of that too, and it doesn't help. Goodbye.'

'Let me know straight away if . . . hello? Malcolm . . .?'

Forty-Three

That'll be the day. Easy to say at dusk with hundreds of ordinary people around, but what about now? What about midnight on a drizzly Monday night a hundred miles from home, jostled by muttering drunks and knots of shouting youths? When the going gets tough the tough get going, but where? Where was she going? What was the point of hurrying in sodden jeans along streets she didn't know? What was she hoping to *find*, for pete's sake? A gingerbread house with a cheerful fire and food on the table and nobody home? A saintly shoe-shop proprietor who'd give her a job and a room and a hundred pounds a week without wanting to know who she was or where she'd come from? Who was she kidding, apart from herself?

There were places open, which surprised her. In Leyford now the shops and eating places would all be locked. No light would spill from their windows. Nobody would walk by. The last pedestrian would have toddled off home an hour ago, leaving the town to the streetlamps and the cats. Here, customers sat in the bright windows of coffee shops and kebab houses as though it were midday, and there were as many people on the street as you'd get on a moderately busy weekday afternoon in Leyford. Trouble was, they weren't the same sort of people. Back home, she'd have attracted attention in her sodden state, even in daylight. There was a good chance somebody would have stopped her by now to ask if she was all right. Not here, though. Here nobody spared her so much as a glance except the occasional bold-eyed youth, and she could have done without that sort of attention. Apart from that she was anonymous. Of no interest. One of thousands.

Without thinking, she turned left, leaving the brightness behind her. She was walking along a narrow street of tall, terraced houses whose doorsteps let straight on to the pavement. It was a poorly-lit street, and if she'd been thinking she probably wouldn't have taken it at this time of night. Who knew what sort of person might be lurking in these shadows, waiting for somebody just like her? Who behind those dark curtained windows would make it their business to come to her rescue if she were attacked? If she'd been thinking, she'd have known the answer to that one.

Plodding with her head down, she became aware that a house ahead of her and on the other side was showing a light. Drawing level she glanced across, swiping rat-tails of dripping hair from her brow. The house door stood open, and a lamp shone on to a board fixed to the wall beside it. SAMARITANS. Annabel pulled a face. Samaritans was for people who were thinking of committing suicide, not runaway teenagers who happened to be cold and wet and scared right now, but who'd be perfectly okay in the morning. It was no fun, what she was doing, but she was a million miles away from killing herself. She'd go home if she ever got *that* desperate.

Mind you ... They'd have a lavatory in there somewhere and she was bursting for a pee. Surely they wouldn't turn her away if she asked to go. They *were* Samaritans, after all. They might even let het dry her hair and give her a cup of tea. And if they wouldn't ... well, there was a nice dry lobby between the open outer door and the closed plate glass one beyond. If they wouldn't let her in she'd spend the rest of the night there. It wouldn't be warm but it'd be dry, and there'd be human beings close by – harmless human beings who weren't asleep. She crossed the street.

Forty-Four

The Sergeant glanced up, his ball-point poised over the page. 'So your daughter packed a bag before she left, sir?'

Malcolm nodded, straining to conceal his impatience.

'And took her savings with her?'

'Yes, I *told* you. Some of her clothes have gone, and all her money. Why is that so important? She's fifteen and she's out there in the dark. *That's* what's important.'

The Sergeant nodded. 'I understand that, sir, believe me. The fact that Annabel packed a bag is important because it suggests she planned her departure beforehand and left of her own free will. In other words we're probably not looking at an abduction, which is something to be thankful for. If it's any consolation I can tell you that thousands of kids do this sort of thing every year and most of them turn up safe and sound, usually within a few days.' He jotted something down. 'You've checked relatives and friends, I suppose?'

'Those who have phones, yes. What are *you* going to do, Sergeant? Apart from writing in that book, I mean?'

'We'll get on to it straight away, sir. Have you a recent photograph of your daughter?'

'There's one taken at school a couple of months ago. D'you want it tonight?'

'Yes, we do, sir, but we'll follow you home and collect it. We'll want to take a look at Annabel's room, anyway. I know you said she didn't leave a note, but there might be something.' He closed the ledger. 'You go out to your car, sir. Our chaps will be right behind you.'

Forty-Five

There was an illuminated bellpush beside the inner door. Annabel hesitated, peering along the brightly-lit corridor beyond the glass. There were two closed doors to the left and a staircase at the end. She shrugged and thumbed the bell. At once the nearer of the two doors opened and an elderly man emerged, wearing brown cord trousers and a fawn cardigan with elbow patches. He wore wire-framed glasses, and except for white tufts over his ears, was bald. He smiled at Annabel through the glass as he operated the lock.

'I'm John,' he said. 'My colleague Mary is in the other room. How might we help you?'

Annabel felt herself flush. 'Well, actually I could do with a lavatory if that's . . .'

'Of course.' The man stepped aside and indicated the staircase. 'Sharp left at the top and it's the door at the end. I'll be in here.' He nodded towards the room he'd emerged from.

In the bathroom she thought, they're good. My colleague Mary is in the other room. That was to let me know I wasn't alone in the place with a man. She smiled at herself in the mirror. Not that I'd be worried if I *was*. Not with John. She washed her hands and face, towelled her head and combed her hair. She wasn't sure what she ought to do next. Her first day in London hadn't been a spectacular success but she certainly wasn't suicidal. Perhaps she should thank the old man for the use of the bathroom and leave. On the other hand it was twenty to one in the morning and she was wet through. Maybe they'd let her change. She wasn't crazy about her uniform and it might still be a bit damp, but it'd be dryer than what she had on now. She'd go down and play it by ear.

John was standing on a worn green carpet with his back to an electric fire. He glanced at Annabel's sport bag. 'You're wet through, my dear. Have you no dry clothing with you?'

Annabel nodded. 'Yes. Well . . .' She smiled. 'Dry*ish*. May I go back upstairs and change?'

He smiled. 'You may, of course, but if these clothes of yours are only dry*ish*, it might be better that we lend you some dry ones.' He moved away from the fire. 'Stand here where it's warm while I fetch Mary.'

The heat felt good. She had actually begun to steam by the time the woman appeared. 'Hello, dear. Sorry to keep you waiting. I was on the phone. I'm Mary, by the way.'

Mary's voice was brisk without being unfriendly. She was slim, somewhere in the forties with well-cut, greying hair and an expensive-looking jersey suit in mauve. She looked Annabel up and down. 'My goodness, you *are* wet, aren't you? You'll catch pneumonia if we don't watch out.' She smiled. 'You stay there and steam while I find you something comfy. Shan't be a minute, I promise.'

Forty-Six

'Where *is* she, Malcolm?' Suzanne Henshaw lay on her back, gazing at the disc of light cast on the ceiling by her bedside lamp. '*That's* what I keep asking myself.'

Her husband sighed. 'I wish I could tell you, Suzanne, I really do, but I can't. The police have her picture. We've done all we can for tonight. It's half-past one and I really think you should try to get some sleep. You know what the doctor said.'

'Where's *Annabel* sleeping?' pursued Suzanne. 'Can the doctor tell me *that*?'

'Don't be ridiculous, Suzanne, how *can* he? How can *anybody*? She might be *anywhere* by now.'

'Exactly – and you expect me to *sleep*. I *can't* sleep, and I certainly wouldn't be able to if I were you.'

'What does *that* mean?'

'You *know* what it means, Malcolm. If it wasn't for your obsession with this coven of so-called Little Children, *our* little child would be asleep in her own bed tonight, not wandering about at the mercy of any pervert she happens to run into.' She snorted. 'Where are they now, your Little Children? Your

Brothers and Sisters? Where's Pastor Ken? Out searching, are they?'

'I'm not out searching *myself*, am I?' countered her husband. 'You can hardly expect *them* to be out if *I'm* not. And anyway they don't know she's missing. They'll rally round when they do, you'll see.'

Suzanne shook her head on the pillow. 'I'll tell you exactly what they'll do, Malcolm. They'll do what their sort *always* do in the teeth of somebody else's crisis. They'll pray for you. It doesn't cost anything, and they don't have to tramp about in the rain.'

'You've become a cynic, Suzanne. Have you taken your tablet?'

'You've become pathetic, Malcolm. Have you taken leave of your senses?'

Forty-Seven

'I expect *that* feels a bit better, dear.' Mary gathered up Annabel's discarded clothes as the girl pulled down a warm jumper over a skirt which was only slightly too wide in the waist. 'Sit by the fire. I'll spread these to dry upstairs, then make us both a cup of tea. Are you hungry?'

'Starving,' Annabel smiled. 'You're being terrifically kind, er . . .'

'Mary. My name's Mary.'

'Mary. You're being very kind, and you don't even *know* me.'

The woman shrugged. 'That's what we're here for, dear. We don't know *any* of the people who come to us – not even their first names, unless they want to tell us.'

'Oh – I don't mind your knowing mine. It's Annabel.'

'Well, Annabel, you sit down and I'll fetch tea and biscuits. Then if you like we can have a little chat.'

Mary went out, closing the door behind her. Annabel sat down in a battered armchair – part of a three-piece suite whose mustard upholstery clashed with the green of the carpet. I suppose people donate furniture and stuff, she thought. And clothes. She felt snug in her borrowed outfit. A thought came. How'll Mum be feeling right now? She suppressed it, studying the faded blue curtains which concealed the room's large window.

Mary came back with a laden tray. John had opened the door for her. He smiled at Annabel over Mary's shoulder, then returned to the other room. Annabel started to get up to close the door, but Mary pushed it shut with her bottom. 'Here we are, dear – hot tea and digestives. We don't keep anything more substantial, I'm afraid.'

'Oh, no – this is fine.' Annabel took the proffered mug, wrapping her hands round it though they weren't cold, now. 'I don't want to eat you out of house and home.'

Mary chuckled. 'Dig in, dear. It's only a plate of biscuits.' She sat back in the other armchair, sipping tea, watching Annabel through the steam. Annabel ate a biscuit, trying not to gobble. Mary sat perfectly still. Annabel took a second digestive, then a third, thinking, when I get work I'll come back here, bring some biscuits. She looked at Mary, who was gazing into the fire.

'I – feel like a fraud.'

Mary looked across. A quizzical look. She didn't speak.

'I mean . . .' Annabel pulled a face. 'I'm not suicidal or anything. You're supposed to be suicidal, aren't you, to come to Samaritans?'

Mary smiled and shook her head. 'Not necessarily,

Annabel. Most people we see just want somebody to talk to.'

'What about?'

The woman shrugged. 'Anything. Their lives. Their thoughts. Their problems. Life's so fast nowadays, people don't have time to listen.' She smiled. 'That's where we come in.'

'I – I ran away from home,' said Annabel. 'This morning,' She looked at her watch. '*Yesterday* morning, I suppose it is now.' She hadn't *meant* to tell Mary this. It just came out.

Mary nodded. 'I see. Things bad at home, I suppose?'

Annabel looked down, biting her lip. Mary leaned forward and touched her elbow. 'You don't have to tell me if you'd rather not. You don't have to tell me *anything* at all, Annabel. We can just sit, or I can leave you alone for a while.'

'No.' Annabel shook her head. 'I don't want to be left alone. I want to tell you about it if I'm not being a nuisance.'

'Of *course* you're not being a nuisance, Annabel. I told you – I'm *here* to listen. You can tell me anything you want to. Anything at all.'

'You'll think I'm *awful*, doing this to Mum when she's . . .' Annabel surprised herself by bursting into tears, and then Mary was kneeling, taking away the mug, hugging her as she hadn't been hugged since she was a little girl.

Forty-Eight

'. . . Anyway it was the final straw, you know? Dragging me off like that in front of my friends. In front of Mig. Does that sound daft?'

Mary shook her head. 'No, Annabel. Not daft. It doesn't strike me as the *worst* thing that's happened to you – having to withdraw from your courses at school seems worse to me, but then I'm older and I wasn't *there*.' She nodded. 'I can certainly see why you ran away. The question is, what now? I mean, you've already found out it's no picnic in London, and the fact that you're only fifteen doesn't help. In the eyes of the law, you're too young to strike out on your own. The police are almost certainly looking for you.'

Annabel gazed at her. 'You won't turn me in, will you? I *can't* go back. Not yet. Not till Dad gets over . . . whatever it is that's got hold of him. You *do* understand, don't you?'

Mary nodded, looking away. 'Yes, Annabel. I understand. And of course I won't turn you in. The Samaritans treat what they're told in strictest confidence, always. But there *is* a problem.' She looked at her watch. 'It's four in the morning. We're not running a bed and breakfast hotel. According to the rules I ought to let you go now, but it's far too late to find you a bed in a hostel.' She sighed. 'If you were sixteen I'd suggest you go to the nearest police station and ask them to let you sit in reception till daylight for your own safety, but of course if *you* did that you'd be taken home.'

Annabel made to rise. 'I *am* being a nuisance, Mary. I know I am. My stuff'll be dry by now. You've done your best for me. Why don't I just change and go?'

'No. No, sit down please, Annabel. I'm going to go through and talk to John for a minute. It's completely against the rules, but I've had an idea.' She got up. 'I shan't be long. Why don't you lie down on the sofa and get a bit of sleep? There's a rug in the corner cupboard. Wrap yourself in that.'

Forty-Nine

There were springs sticking up in the sofa and Annabel didn't expect to sleep, but when she woke the blue curtain had been pulled back to admit daylight and Mary was joggling her shoulder.

'I'm sorry to wake you, dear, but I'm off duty in a minute and we must go.'

'We?' Annabel knuckled her eyes and sat up, raking her fingers through her hair.

Mary nodded. 'I'm taking you home for a spot of breakfast, then you'll have to decide whether you want to move on or stay at my place.'

'Stay? You mean . . .?'

'John and I had a long talk, Annabel, and I've decided to offer you a room, but there are conditions.'

'What sort of conditions?'

'Well, first of all, you must understand that I'm making this offer as a private citizen and not in my capacity as a Samaritan volunteer. That's *extremely* important. If word got around that volunteers offer accommodation in their own homes, it would cause tremendous difficulties for the organisation. Volunteers *don't*, and I must ask you never to tell anybody that they do.'

'Okay. What are the other conditions?'

'There are two others, Annabel. One is that you are to regard your stay in London as a strictly *temporary* arrangement. Not just your stay with *me*, but your stay in London. I understand why you ran away, but if you're going to live at my house you must promise me that after a time you'll go home and give it another try. Will you do that?'

'I . . . as long as you don't mean three days or something. I mean, nothing's going to change in three days, is it?'

Mary pulled a face. 'Even three days will seem like forever to your parents, Annabel, believe me. Which brings us neatly to my third and final condition.'

'Which is?'

'That you phone home the *minute* we get to my place.'

'*What?*' Annabel leapt up. 'You're joking. What's the point of telling them where I am after *one night*? Dad'd be down here like a ferret down a rathole, dragging me home. No thanks. Give me my stuff and I'll go.'

'Now wait a minute.' Mary's hand circled her wrist. 'Simmer down, Annabel. I said nothing about telling your parents where you *are*. All I want you to tell them is that you're safe and well and staying with a friend. You needn't even say London. It won't be like having you back, but at least they won't lie in bed at night imagining you on the street in the rain or lying dead in a ditch somewhere.

That's the worst part. That's the bit you've no right to inflict on them, no matter *what* they've done. Believe me – I *know*.'

Annabel looked at her. 'Did someone . . .?'

'Yes, Annabel, someone did. Someone very dear to me.' She smiled tightly. 'I suppose that's why I'm taking you home with me. You know – in the hope that somebody somewhere has done the same for him. Anyway, what I want to know is, will you make that call?'

Annabel hesitated, then nodded. 'Okay. But I won't be doing it for *him*. It'll be for Mum and Sarah.'

'That's absolutely fine, Annabel.' Mary smiled. 'And now let's get that breakfast. You must be famished.'

Fifty

'Your mother's not getting up this morning, Sarah. She didn't sleep last night.'

Sarah shook her head. 'I didn't either, Dad. I kept thinking about Annabel outside in the dark. When d'you think she'll come home?'

'I don't know, sweetheart. I've asked the Lord to take care of her for us, and He will.'

'I hope so. I asked Him too, over and over.'

'Good girl. I want you to take Mummy's tray up and tell her you'll be staying at home today to look after her. I'll phone school so they won't expect you.'

Sarah carried the tray upstairs. Her mother, propped on pillows, looked washed out. She managed a wan smile. 'Good morning, darling. Waiting on Mummy hand and foot as usual.'

Sarah smiled. 'It's nothing, Mummy. Daddy says I'm to stay at home today to look after you. He's calling school. And he says you're to eat *all* of your breakfast.'

Suzanne looked at the tray. It supported a bowl of cornflakes, a boiled egg, some buttered toast and a cup of tea. She pulled a face. 'I'll probably manage some tea and toast, darling. I'm not sure about the cornflakes, though, or the egg.' She looked at her daughter. 'You've been crying.'

Sarah nodded. 'All night, just about. Where's she *gone*, Mummy? Where is Annabel *now*? It feels funny without her.'

Suzanne nodded, suppressing a sniffle. 'I know, darling, but you mustn't worry. Annabel's a sensible girl. She'll be all right, you'll see.' She forced a smile. 'I expect she'll be back in a day or two, none the worse for her adventure.'

Sarah was on the bottom step when the phone rang. She snatched it up. 'Leyford 646242, Sarah speaking.'

'Hi, kiddo. It's me.'

'ANNABEL? Where are you? Are you all *right*? When're you coming *home*?'

'I don't know. Listen. Tell Mum I'm well and staying with a friend. Tell her not to worry – nothing bad's going to happen to me. Okay?'

'Yes, but hold on a sec, Annabel – Dad's coming. He wants . . .'

'No way, kiddo. Watch yourself with those friends of his. 'Bye.'

'Give me that.' Malcolm grabbed the receiver. 'Annabel, I know it's you. Where . . . hello? Hello? Annabel?'

Sarah left him to it and bounded up the stairs. 'Mum! Mum, it's Annabel! She phoned. She's OK, Mum. MUM . . .'

Fifty-One

Mary popped her head round the door as Annabel hung up 'Did you get through, dear?'

Annabel nodded. 'Yes, thanks.'

'Who did you speak to?'

'Sarah.'

'Your sister?'

'That's right.'

Mary smiled. 'I expect she was happy to hear from you.'

'Yes.' Annabel nodded. 'She asked where I was and when I was coming home. I didn't tell her, but she'll tell Mum I'm OK.' She pulled a face. 'Dad came on just as I was hanging up. He'll be praise the Lording all over the place. They always praise the Lord, never the people who actually *do* something – people like you.'

Mary shrugged. 'Perhaps they believe God works *through* those people, Annabel.' She smiled. 'Breakfast's just about ready if you'd like to come through.'

Fifty-Two

'Hello? Is this the Pastor?'

'Speaking.'

'Malcolm, Pastor. Malcolm Henshaw.'

'Oh, good morning, Malcolm. Call me Ken, for goodness' sake. How can I help you?'

'I – don't really know, Ken. What's happened is, my daughter's run away.'

'Little Sarah?'

'Oh, no. My elder daughter, Annabel. There was some unpleasantness between us last Friday when I forbade her to go to the Mall to see a pop singer open a shop. She said hurtful things to me and locked herself in her room, and then on Saturday morning she slipped out before anybody else was up.'

'And . . . disappeared?'

'No. Not then. She'd gone to the Mall. As soon as I realised, I went down there and dragged her home. I . . . lost my temper, I suppose.'

'And then what happened?'

'Well – I grounded her, Ken. Confined her to her room. She stayed there all day Sunday but she must have packed a bag. She set off for school yesterday as usual and never arrived. We didn't know till teatime, then we discovered that some of her clothes had gone, together with her savings.'

'Hmmm. And you've heard nothing since?'

'Oh, yes. She phoned a couple of hours ago, spoke to Sarah. Safe with a friend, she says.'

'Praise the Lord.'

'But she didn't say *where*, or when she'll be back. Her mother's extremely upset, which doesn't help in her condition. I don't know what to *do*, Ken. I'm afraid I was a bit hard on Annabel.'

'No.'

'Pardon?'

'You weren't *hard*, Malcolm. You were exercising your prerogative as a parent, that's all. Rooting out an occasion of wrong living. You mustn't blame yourself.'

'But she's *gone*, Ken. My daughter's left home and she's only fifteen.'

'What a blessing, though, Malcolm, to know she's safe and well.'

'Yes, I know, but . . .'

'Remember the Prodigal Son, Malcolm. He too left home taking all his money, but he returned chastened to the fold when he'd spent it all. Annabel will come home, and her call tells us that in the meantime the Lord is providing for her, as He provided for the five thousand in the parable of the loaves and fishes.'

'I – suppose you're right, Ken. Things could be much worse, and I certainly feel better now that we've talked. Thank you.'

'Don't thank *me*, Malcolm – thank the Lord. We

must trust in Him with the simple, unquestioning trust of little children. Nothing more is required of us.'

'I *know* you're right, Ken. I can *feel* it.'

'Goodbye then, Malcolm, till this evening.'

'Goodbye. And thanks again.'

Fifty-Three

'More toast, dear?'

'Oooh, no, thanks, Mary. I'm stuffed.'

'Well – I have to dash, I'm afraid, but you sit and digest a while. Read the paper. Have more coffee – there's plenty.' She stood up. 'I ought to be back around four.'

Annabel looked at her. 'You mean you're going to leave me here in your place by myself?'

Mary smiled. 'I suppose you could come with me if you wanted to, but you'd be bored silly. I do reception work along at the Medical Centre. It's a very nice Centre, but you wouldn't want to spend six hours in it waiting for somebody.'

Annabel shook her head. 'I didn't mean *that*, Mary. I don't mind being left, but how d'you know I won't nick all your stuff and go off?'

The woman smiled again. 'I'm a fair judge of character, Annabel. If you nick my stuff while I'm gone, I'll pose topless for a week in Harrod's window. How's that?'

Annabel grinned. 'Thanks, Mary. I guess you know I'd like to stay here, but I *really* don't want to be a pest. Is there anything I can do to help while you're gone?'

'Certainly, dear. You can wash the breakfast things and put them away. Look in all the cupboards – you'll soon learn where everything goes. Oh – and you could have the kettle on when I get back. *That*'d be nice. Okay?'

The washing up didn't take long, and she found the cutlery drawer and the crockery cupboard and a row of hooks for beakers and a rail with tea towels on it. Mary keeps a tidy house, she thought. Except that it wasn't a house. Not a whole one. It was half a house. Mary had the first and second floors. Somebody else had the ground floor and area. Who, wondered Annabel. No noise from down there. At work, probably. Whoever it was, you passed their door in the dim hallway just before the stairs up to Mary's.

She explored. The first floor consisted of the kitchen-cum-breakfast room, a big sitting-room with lots of old furniture and a pair of glazed doors that opened on to a tiny balcony, and a bathroom. Upstairs were two bedrooms, one bigger than the other, and a tiny office with a battered desk and a steel filing-cabinet. The larger bedroom was obviously Mary's. It had a double bed and smelt of her scent. On a bedside unit was a framed photograph of a man and a boy of about eight. Annabel picked it up and took it over to the window. Both subjects were smiling broadly. The man was wearing a check shirt open at the neck. The little boy had on a check shirt too, and looked quite a lot like Mary. It was probably one of these two who walked out of

Mary's life ... how long ago? And where's the other? She shrugged and put the photo back on the unit.

The other bedroom had a single bed with a unit like Mary's, a chest of drawers and two wardrobes; one fitted, the other free-standing. The chest and free-standing wardrobe were empty. The fitted one was locked. The bright wallpaper had hundreds of pinholes as though the walls had once been decked with posters.

This'll be my room, mused Annabel. Or rather it'll be the one I sleep in. It won't be mine. It's got a feel to it. An atmosphere, like – like waiting. That's it. This room's *waiting*. She lifted a corner of net curtain and saw a jumble of rooftops stretching into misty distance. It's a waiting room, she told herself, letting the net fall. And I'm not the one it's waiting for.

Fifty-Four

'Hello, Mary. How was your day?'

Mary grinned, hanging up her coat. 'You sound like a wife, dear. My day was distinctly average, thank you.' She turned. 'And you – you decided not to abscond with my possessions after all?'

'Just as you predicted,' smiled Annabel. 'Tea's brewing, by the way.'

'That's what I like to hear.'

They sat at the kitchen table sipping hot tea. 'So,' said Mary, 'what did you find to do all day?'

'I explored the house,' admitted Annabel. 'I hope you don't mind.'

'Mind?' Mary shook her head. 'Why should I mind, dear? There are no concealed bodies. No stolen goods. It's just a boring little flat full of boring bits and pieces.' She smiled. 'How do you like your room?'

'What? Oh, the little bedroom. It's lovely. I . . .'

Mary raised her eyebrows. 'You were about to say something else, dear. What was it?'

Annabel looked into her tea. 'Nothing, really. I was going to say I call it the waiting room.'

'The *waiting* room? Why the waiting room, Annabel?'

'Because it's waiting. I mean, I got a feeling when I was in there, as though the room was waiting for something, or somebody.' She giggled. 'Now you'll think I'm barmy.'

'Not at all.' Mary had put down her beaker and was gazing at Annabel. 'Psychic, perhaps. Not barmy.' She sighed. 'Were there any phone calls while I was out?'

'Oh, no – I'd have told you straight away. Why – were you expecting . . .?'

'No, no. Not expecting, dear.' She forced a grin. 'Waiting. Like the room.'

Annabel looked up. 'There's a photo . . .'

'Yes. The man's my husband. Was, I should say. He met somebody he liked better. The child's my son. We're waiting for *him*, the room and I.'

'Where . . .?'

'Where *is* he?' Mary shook her head. 'I don't know, Annabel. He ran away one day when he was fifteen and I haven't heard from him since.' She sighed again. 'Eight years, waiting for the phone to ring.'

'I'm sorry,' murmured Annabel. 'I shouldn't have . . .'

'It's all right, dear. I've got used to it. It's become a part of my life, but now you know why I offered to take you in, and why I insisted you phone home.'

Annabel nodded. 'I wish . . . I hope . . . what's his name, Mary?'

'Neil. His name's Neil, and perhaps he *will* call one of these days. Meanwhile.' She smiled. 'D'you think we might squeeze a few more drops out of that pot?'

Fifty-Five

Sarah was chopping lettuce in the kitchen when her father got in. It was ten to six. 'Hello, sweetheart. How's Mum?'

Sarah pulled a face. 'She keeps crying, Dad. She's in the front room.'

He went through. Suzanne was dabbing her cheek with a tissue. He knelt beside her chair and took her hand. 'You mustn't cry, my love. Annabel *will* come home, and as Pastor Ken pointed out at least we know she's safe, and that's a blessing.'

'You've seen him?'

'Phoned him. This morning. He's praying for us.'

'He will be. Did you tell him *why* she ran away?'

'I did, and he said I mustn't blame myself. He mentioned the Prodigal Son, who came home when his money ran out. He said Annabel will do the same, and that in the meantime the Lord is providing for her as He provided for the five thousand in the parable of the Loaves and Fishes.' He looked at her. 'Perhaps if *you* were to pray . . .'

'D'you think I *haven't* prayed, Malcolm? I'm praying all the time but she's not here, and unlike you I can't find comfort in the words of a supposed priest who thinks Loaves and Fishes is a parable.'

'What d'you mean?'

'Loaves and Fishes is not a parable, Malcolm. It's an account of something Jesus *did*. One of His miracles. You'd think a Pastor would know that, wouldn't you?'

'Well . . .' He let go her hand and ran his fingers through his hair, looking at the carpet. 'I expect it was a slip of the tongue, Suzanne. Just a slip of the tongue, that's all.' He gazed at her. 'Why do you fight me? Can't you see I'm doing this for *you*? Struggling to eliminate wrong living from our lives so that you'll get better?'

His wife smiled sadly. 'I know that's what you *believe*, my dear. That man has made you believe it, just as he's made you believe there were never any cavemen, even though you once stood beside me in a Spanish cave and admired their paintings. He's closed your mind, Malcolm. It's what these people *do*.'

'*These people*.' He stood up. 'You make them sound like a secret society or something. They're Christians, Suzanne, that's all. Christians trying to live as Jesus wanted us to live.'

His wife shook her head. 'They're bigots, Malcolm. Bigots with closed minds. They can do nothing for you, and they *certainly* can't do anything for me.' She looked up at him. 'Why don't you go and give Sarah a hand with the meal? I believe I could manage a little of the soup if nothing else.'

Fifty-Six

Over the next week, Annabel settled in at Mary's. Her friend bought her clothes, shoes and a Millennium poster to cover some of the pinholes on her wall. When Mary was on duty, either at the health centre or the Samaritans, Annabel cooked, cleaned and answered the phone. Each time she picked up the phone she hoped the caller would be Mary's son, but it never was.

One afternoon over tea, Annabel said, 'I've been thinking, Mary. I can't sponge on you for ever, and I really feel I should earn my keep. I'd like to try for a Saturday job.'

'Hooo! You'll be lucky, my love. There're hundreds looking for Saturday work. Thousands, I shouldn't wonder. And anyway, you don't need a job. You do a wonderful job here, and you know you've only to ask if you need anything.'

Annabel nodded. 'I know, but I don't like cadging off you. You do enough for me without that. I want my own money.'

The woman smiled. 'Well, there's no harm in trying, I suppose.' She gazed at the girl. 'But don't start putting down roots, Annabel. There's your family to consider. Especially your mother. Don't you think it might aggravate her illness, worrying about you?'

Annabel lowered her gaze. 'I . . . guess it might. What if I was to phone again – tell her I'm okay? It wouldn't be so bad then, would it?'

Mary pulled a face. 'It would make her feel a *bit* better, I suppose. But you must go home soon – give it another try.'

'I know. I'm sorry, Mary. It's just . . . I don't think it's been long enough. Things won't have changed. If I go back to the same situation I'll only leave again. I must stay till December.'

Mary sighed. 'That's far too long, Annabel. Not for me – I love your being here – but for your family. No, Annabel, it really won't do. I told you when I brought you here that this was a strictly temporary arrangement. I'm going to suggest a compromise. The end of the month. October 31st.'

'That's not much of a compromise,' cried Annabel. 'Three more weeks instead of two months. You might as well make me go now.'

Mary nodded. 'That's what I ought to do, my dear, but there it is: three weeks or nothing. Which is it to be?'

'I . . . I'll take the three weeks. And thanks. You've been fantastic.'

'And you'll phone home?'

'Yes, of course. I . . . like you a lot, Mary.'

'I know. I like you, too. Off you go now and make that call. And then you can have a go at finding a job. It won't be easy.'

Fifty-Seven

Annabel walked into the shopping centre just after eight. Smith's was open for papers. Everything else was locked and shuttered. An old homeless man watched her from his seat on a bench under a weeping fig. Bottles of milk stood outside some of the shops. Beyond the escalator with its curtain of falling water a smart manageress was unlocking the metal grille across a jeweller's window.

None of the shops was advertising vacancies. Annabel scanned them all till only Island was left. She'd been amazed the first time she'd come here to find a coffee shop identical to the one on the Mall back home, right down to the name. She'd always assumed Island was locally owned, but it was obviously part of a chain.

A middle-aged woman in a green overall and white hat was moving among the tables with a cloth, wiping surfaces and adjusting the positions of chairs. Annabel stood till the woman noticed her and straightened up. 'We're not open yet, dear. Half-past.'

'I know. I was wondering . . .'

'Looking for a job, are you?'

'Yes. Just Saturdays. I'm still at school.'

'Ah.' The woman came over. 'How old are you, dear?'

'Fifteen.'

'And do your parents know you're looking for work?'

'Oh, yes.'

'Ah-ha. Start straight away, could you?'

'You mean there's a job *now* – today?'

'Yes, dear, there is. I'll give you a try, but I'll expect you to work. I won't pay you to stand around gossiping with your friends. That's what the last girl did.'

'I won't do that.' Fat chance, she thought. I *have* no friends, and if I had they wouldn't come a hundred miles for coffee. She looked at the woman. 'What *is* the pay, please?'

'One-fifty an hour, eight till four-thirty, hour off for lunch. Comes to eleven-fifty.'

Annabel's eyes widened. 'Eleven pounds fifty – just for a day?'

The woman nodded, smiling. 'You'll earn it, deary, make no mistake. Come four-thirty your feet'll be killing you. You'll just want to fall into bed.'

At eight-twenty, kitted out in cap and overall, Annabel found herself stacking rolls in baskets on the servery. She could hardly believe it. She knew she'd been fantastically lucky, but her joy wasn't completely unrestrained. She'd lied to her employer. Misled her about school and parents. She'd certainly get the sack if it ever came out. And she hadn't said she'd be leaving in a few weeks. Still. Little white lies, right? You've got to tell 'em sometimes. Everybody does.

Fifty-Eight

The Manageress was called Mrs North and she was right. By mid-afternoon the soles of Annabel's feet throbbed and burned and there was an ache in the small of her back from bending over tables. Customers came and went in a never-ending blur; grousing, touching her in sly ways and leaving drifts of crumbs and sticky splashes which made her wonder what their tablecloths at home were like. Time passed so slowly she thought it was standing still, and when her employer put out the CLOSED board at four-fifteen she could have wept with relief.

'Now, dear,' said Mrs North when Annabel had put the chairs on the tables, swept and mopped the floor and put the chairs down again. 'How've you got on?'

Annabel clawed damp hair from her forehead and smiled. 'Okay, I think. Was I all right?'

The woman nodded. 'You've done very well. 'T'isn't easy money, though, is it?'

Annabel shook her head. 'No, but I'll get used to it. Can I come next week?'

''Course you can, dear. Eight o'clock sharp. Here y'are.' She peeled two fivers off a wad, wrapped them round some coins and handed them over.

'Thanks,' smiled Annabel. 'Saturday, then.'

The woman nodded. 'You'll be stiff tomorrow, dear. Let me know if you get second thoughts, won't you? Don't just not turn up.'

Annabel shook her head. 'I wouldn't do that, and anyway I won't have second thoughts. Bye.'

'Bye, Annabel.'

The short walk back to Mary's was excruciating. Her money was in her jacket pocket and she kept her hand wrapped round it, deriving comfort from the feel of it. Mary was in the kitchen, looking as worn-out as Annabel felt.

She smiled. 'Did you find work?'

'Yeah.' Annabel flopped into a chair. 'Island.' She sighed and shook her head. 'Are most people pigs, or does that coffee shop attract a certain type?'

Mary chuckled. 'It takes all sorts, Annabel. The main thing is, you got a job! I think we should eat out tonight. Celebrate.'

Annabel looked at her. 'Okay, on one condition.'

'What's that?'

'My treat.'

Fifty-Nine

'Malcolm tells me you've heard from Annabel again, my dear.' Malcolm's mother put the tray on the coffee table and handed Suzanne her beaker. Suzanne nodded. 'Yes, but she still won't say where she *is*. She says she's all right, but I *wish* she'd come home.'

'Of course you do, darling, and so do I. I can't help feeling I'm in some way *responsible*. She came to me for help and I couldn't give it. All I could think to do was try to explain Malcolm to her, which really meant finding excuses for him.' She shook her head. 'There *are* no excuses. You got a strange man when you married my Malcolm, Suzanne.'

Suzanne smiled. 'He *is* odd in some ways, Mum, but I knew that before we married, and we were happy enough till this happened. You're not to blame in any way and you mustn't think it. It's that Pastor and his little band of disciples *I* hold responsible. They give me the creeps.'

The older woman looked at her. 'Have you *met* them? I didn't know . . .'

'Some of them. The Pastor called, and a couple called Lynn and Stephen who have a kid called Andrew.' She laughed briefly. 'He was the worst, actually. Eight years old and he says to me, Sister, have you let Jesus into your life? *Sister*, for heaven's sake, and he'd never clapped eyes on me till that moment.' She shivered. 'The most worrying thing is, Sarah's sort of adopted the little monster. Thinks he's sweet. I'm terrified she's going to end up like him, Mum. Him and his brainwashed little automaton friends.'

'No.' The woman shook her head. 'She's bright, Suzanne. If these characters are as ghastly as you say they are, Sarah will see through them soon enough. I wouldn't worry.'

'I can't help . . .' Suzanne broke off as powerful beams swept across the curtain. 'They're back.' They listened. The engine faded as the Renault rolled into the garage. The kitchen door opened. Sarah came hurrying along the hallway and stuck her head round the door. She was flushed. Her eyes sparkled.

'Hey, Mum, Grandma, guess what?' The women smiled, waiting. 'I'm off to Faith Camp on Saturday with Andrew and Fiona and all the other kids. A whole week. I can hardly wait.'

Sixty

'A week?' Sarah's grandma looked at her. 'What about school, darling?'

'It's half-term, Grandma. They wouldn't organise a camp in term time.'

'Of *course* they wouldn't, my love — how silly of me. Where is it to be, this camp?'

'Eden Vale, they call it. It's got woods and streams and everything. Fiona says it's special when we're there because Jesus comes too. You can't *see* Him of course, but you can *feel* Him. That's what Fiona says.'

'Does she, darling? Well, I'm sure you'll have a lovely time.'

The child went to hang up her coat. 'See what I mean?' murmured Suzanne, as Malcolm joined them.

His mother nodded. 'Eden Vale. Isn't that a cheese spread or something?'

Her son looked at her. 'What's that, Mother?'

'Eden Vale, dear. I was saying it sounds like a cheese spread.'

'Oh — Sarah's told you, then. I hope you didn't say that to *her*. She can't wait to get there.'

'Of *course* I didn't, Malcolm.' She looked at him.

'I suppose you realise Suzanne's not wildly keen on Sarah's new friends?'

'I know, Mother, but then Suzanne doesn't really know them. They're lovely kids. Quiet. Clean. Polite. You don't get many like them nowadays, more's the pity.'

'What's the supervision like, dear?'

'Supervision?'

'At these Faith Camps. Who's in charge?'

'Oh, Pastor Ken's in charge, with a couple of the Deacons to assist, and a handful of parents. It's all very well-regulated, Mother, I can assure you.'

'Well, I certainly hope so, darling. One missing daughter is one too many in my opinion. Which reminds me .. what are the police *doing* about Annabel?'

Her son shrugged. 'Very little, since I told them about her call last week. They seem to take the view that since she's obviously in no danger, it isn't really their pigeon. I asked how they knew she wasn't being detained against her will – that somebody wasn't *forcing* her to make the calls. Most unlikely, they said. So.' He shrugged. 'It seems we can only wait, and pray.'

'Quite.' His mother pulled herself out of the armchair. 'I'll be off, then.' She bent to kiss Suzanne on the forehead. 'Get plenty of rest, my dear, and try not to fret. I'll see you on Thursday.'

In the hallway she said, 'You know, Malcolm, I'm not sure I ought to be making myself available twice a week so that you can take Sarah along to that place, except I think perhaps you'd go anyway.' She gazed at him. 'Would you?'

He nodded. 'Yes, Mother, I would. It's *for* Suzanne, you see. All for her. Their prayers. Our right living. Haven't you noticed how much better she's looking?'

'Better?' She shook her head. 'I'm sorry, dear, but I can't say I have. How can she be better when she's fretting day and night over Annabel?' She looked hard at her son. 'If I were you I'd stop wasting my time on those people and start spending it with my wife.' Her voice broke as she added, 'While I still had her.'

Sixty-One

Wednesday, six o'clock. Malcolm rolled the Renault into the garage and sat gazing blankly through the windscreen. Thanks to his mother, a sleepless night had preceded a bad day at the office. Her parting shot of the night before had played back over and over for twenty hours and was still playing.

While I still had her. He shivered. It's not *that* bad, he whispered for the thousandth time. It can't be *that* bad. She *has* been looking better. Mum hasn't noticed, that's all. Too busy gossiping. Mocking my faith. *God is not mocked*, Pastor Ken says, and quite right, too. They'll see. They'll soon stop sniggering when Suzanne's her old self again.

His wife smiled from her armchair as he came in the room. She *does* look better. He pecked her cheek. 'How's my girl?'

'Not too bad. Malcolm?'

'Huh?'

'A letter came today. From the hospital.'

'A letter?' His heart kicked as she showed him the crumpled brown envelope. 'What about, Suzanne?'

'They want me in, dear. Next Monday. Chemotherapy.'

'But I thought ... I didn't expect you'd *need*

anything like that, Suzanne. You've been doing so well . . .'

She shook her head. 'I *haven't*, darling. Not really. I try not to moan and groan because moaning does no good, and perhaps I've fooled you without meaning to, but I haven't fooled myself. I *need* the treatment.' She smiled tightly. 'They wouldn't be offering me a bed for a week otherwise, would they, with things as they are?'

He ate Sarah's meal in a sort of daze, then went upstairs and sat on the bed. Our bed, he murmured to his wan reflection in the mirror. *My* bed, it replied, and tears sprang from his eyes. *We must trust in Him with the simple, unquestioning trust of little children.* Yes, I know, but it's so *hard*, because Annabel was right. The ponies *were* still in the field. I remember. Nothing changed, did it, except inside my head?

A sign. I need a sign. I know it's supposed to be blasphemous or sacrilegious or something to ask for your own personal sign from God, but what's wrong with needing your faith bolstered? He sends things to *test* it, so why not things to strengthen it now and then as well?

I'm being tested, all right. First Suzanne, then Annabel. All I need now is boils all over my body.

Next Monday. She's going in next Monday. Sarah'll be away at Faith Camp, *if* she'll still go. She might prefer . . . no, it doesn't matter what she prefers, she'll *have* to go. Can't have her here alone

159

all day while I'm at work, can we? In fact it's worked out just . . .

That's it! He gasped, dashing the tears from his eyes with the back of his hand. I asked for a sign and it was here already, only I didn't recognise it. I thought it was coincidence, Faith Camp falling the same week as Suzanne's appointment, but there's no such thing as coincidence, is there? Pastor Ken said that. Everything that happens is part of His plan, he said.

Part of His plan. Malcolm felt his heart lift. We're in His hands. Suzanne and Sarah. Annabel and me. We all fit into the plan. Nothing can happen without His consent, so everything's going to be all right. Praise the Lord!

Sixty-Two

Malcolm stood at the foot of the stairs and called up. 'You ready, Sarah? Coach won't wait.'

'Coming.' His daughter started down with her luggage. The sports bag banged against her leg with every step. Malcolm nodded towards it. 'What've you *got* in there, sweetheart – the kitchen sink?'

She shook her head. 'Just the stuff on the list, Dad.' She paused on the bottom step, gazing at him. 'Do I *have* to go, Dad? *Do* I?'

'You could hardly *wait* a couple of days ago, Sarah. What's wrong all of a sudden?'

'You *know*, Dad. It's Mum. I didn't know she'd be going into hospital, did I? I wouldn't have . . .'

'Listen, sweetheart.' He took hold of her shoulders and looked into her eyes. 'There's nothing to worry about, okay? Your Mum's getting better every day. The doctor thinks a few days in hospital will help her get well more *quickly*, that's all. Come kiss her goodbye, there's a good girl.'

He took the bag and steered Sarah into the living room. Suzanne looked up and smiled. 'All ready, then?'

Sarah nodded. There was an aching lump in her throat and she stared at the carpet to keep from crying, but it was no use. A wail burst out of her and she ran into her mother's arms. 'Oh, Mum,' she choked, 'I don't want to leave you. I *don't*.'

'Hey, now.' Suzanne hugged and rocked, gazing at her husband over a heaving shoulder as she murmured in the child's ear. 'It's all right, darling. Mummy's going to be absolutely fine, I promise, and when you come home I'll be here in this very chair, waiting to hear all about your adventures.'

Sarah wasn't easily comforted, and by the time she'd cried herself out, blown her nose and had her face mopped by her mother it was twenty past eight. She still didn't want to go, but Mum was smiling encouragement and Dad was warming up the Renault. Further resistance would be futile. She kissed her mother and left.

Sixty-Three

When Annabel woke on Sunday morning she felt as though she'd fallen out of a train. Stiff from shoulder to ankle, she decided she'd lie in till ten o'clock at the earliest. She gazed at her Millennium poster, thought about last night at the Chicken Shack and tried not to move.

A hundred miles away Sarah, unused to sleeping on the ground, also woke up stiff. She'd have welcomed a lie-in but there was no chance. At seven o'clock the flap of the tent she was sharing with Fiona was pulled back and Fiona's mum shook them awake.

'Come on, girls, rise and shine.' Her name was Phyllis and she was in charge of the girls' tents. There were eight tents altogether – six small ones for the children and two big ones where the adults slept. The big tents were used in the daytime for indoor activities if the weather was bad.

It wasn't bad this morning. The rising sun glinted through autumn trees as Sarah and Fiona knelt on dewy grass, washing in the bucket of icy water Phyllis had carried from the stream.

'Brrrr!' Sarah sat back on her heels, grabbed a

rough towel and rubbed her face, arms and neck. 'It's flippin' freezing.'

Her companion chuckled. 'You'll get used to it, Sister.' She lifted a dripping face to sniff the air. 'Sausages for breakfast, praise the Lord.'

Sarah pulled on a thick sweater. 'Good. I'm starving.' As she spoke, an insistent clanging broke out. She glanced round. Near the men's tent a large triangle hung from a miniature gallows. Pastor Ken was standing by the gallows with a broad grin on his face, striking the triangle with an iron bar. Fiona jumped up, dragging a comb through her tangled hair. 'Come on Sarah, or we'll be late for morning prayers.' She stuffed the comb in her jeans' pocket and hurried towards the open space at the centre where others were gathering. Sarah bent over her trainer, doing it up as fast as her aching muscles would allow. Never mind prayers, she muttered, what about the *sausages*?

With Pastor Ken and the kids away at camp, the meeting that evening was a subdued affair. Suzanne was due to go into hospital tomorrow and Malcolm had been in two minds about attending. His mother had treated him to one of her withering stares when she'd arrived to sit with her daughter-in-law, but he'd averted his eyes and walked out to the car in pursuit of whatever comfort might be had at the Citadel. In the event, it was scant. Deacon Neil was standing in for Ken. Malcolm had heard him preach before and had been impressed, but this time he seemed almost listless, as though his heart wasn't in the work, and consequently the meeting never came to life.

It's partly me, I suppose, Malcolm told himself. Thinking about tomorrow. Suzanne. He'd mentioned it to somebody before the meeting and at one point Neil led them in a prayer for Suzanne, but Malcolm's feeling as he got into the car at nine o'clock was one of vague disappointment. He thought wistfully of Eden Vale where Sarah was, and Pastor Ken. *That's* where the spirit is tonight, he told himself. Lucky Sarah.

Sixty-Four

The autumn sunlight seemed extra bright after the greenish gloom of the hospital corridor, and as he took the footpath towards the car-park Malcolm tried to feel God looking down on him and the hospital and Suzanne in her high narrow bed, but all he could feel was the aching lump in his throat. An hour ago they'd walked up this path together. What if it had been their *last* walk? The last ever? He hadn't even *thought* about that at the time. He'd wondered how long the admission procedure would take – how late he'd be getting into the office. *That*'ll be a wonderful memory to cherish over the years, won't it, if . . .

No! He shook his head. Don't think like that. That's wrong living. Faith, Malcolm. *The simple, unquestioning faith of little children*. Think about Sarah this lovely morning at Eden Vale, laughing and playing in the sunshine without a care in the world. We're here, Jesus sees us, everything's fine. *That's* the way to live.

As Malcolm walked down the hospital pathway, Pastor Ken was standing on the bank of the stream, staring in horror at the glistening object in his palm.

In front of him, wondering what she'd done to make him so angry, stood a little girl called Rebecca.

'Children – stop what you're doing, please. Gather round.' He waited till they stood barefoot in a semicircle, watching his face. Then he took the object between thumb and forefinger and held it up. 'Who knows what this is?'

Sarah screwed up her eyes to peer at it, then raised her hand.

'Yes, Sarah?'

'I – I think it's an ammonite, Pastor.'

'An ammonite.' Pastor Ken nodded gravely. 'In other words, a type of fossil. And who makes fossils and sows them in the earth, Andrew?'

'Satan, Pastor.'

'Satan.' He frowned down at the trembling Rebecca. 'Child, you are unclean. You have handled an object of Satan's. *I* am unclean, having handled it also. Has anybody else . . .' His eyes flicked from face to face. 'Has anybody else touched this vile object, or one like it?'

Sarah gulped and nodded. 'I – I found one, Pastor. In the stream. I dropped it when – when you . . . it's here in the grass by my foot.'

'DON'T TOUCH IT!' Sarah flinched and withdrew her foot. She'd never known the Pastor to shout. He stared at her till she dropped her eyes. 'You, too, are defiled. Take this little one and wait in the women's tent. We must be purified, and in the meantime . . .' He looked at the others. 'In the meantime, nobody must touch us, speak to us or even *look* at us.' He peered into the trees and spoke softly. 'Satan was here, in this lovely place. He's never far away, wherever we are. We must watch and pray. Watch and pray. Sister Broadbent?'

'Yes, Pastor?' Fiona's mother kept her eyes on the ground.

'Take my place. I will retire to my tent till purification.' He gazed at the ten remaining youngsters. 'Carry on, children. Jesus is here. I feel His presence.'

They dispersed, to play in a subdued way under Sister Broadbent's watchful gaze. The Pastor turned and stalked up the slope. As he passed the women's tent the sound of weeping reached him from within.

Sixty-Five

Tuesday morning, ten o'clock. At the office, Malcolm is speaking with a potential client. Her name is Mrs Trubshaw and she's interested in the semi-detached property on the Wednesfield road, but with her husband at work she doesn't want to make a firm commitment. Malcolm is doing his best, but his mind is elsewhere. The phone rings, making him jump. 'Excuse me.' He picks up.

'Highgate Property Services, Henshaw speaking. Yes, this *is* Malcolm Henshaw. Yes. Is something ... *what?* But I thought she was in for chemotherapy. We were told ... scan? Yes, and ... oh my God! Is it ... I mean is she going to ...? Yes, I'll come at once. About fifteen minutes. Thanks.'

They were kind at the hospital, but firm. They wouldn't let him see Suzanne. The young doctor who came to Reception explained. 'Your wife's just gone down to theatre, Mr Henshaw. The consultant will want to see you as soon as he's free, so if you'll come with me I'll show you where you can sit.' She looked washed out. In a daze, Malcolm followed her along corridors with gleaming floors till she stopped by an open door. 'Here we are, Mr Henshaw. Have a seat. I'll get somebody to bring you a cup of tea. Okay?' Malcolm nodded dumbly and she hurried off.

There were chairs round three walls but he had the room to himself. It was pink. He sat like a man in a trance. No tea came. He counted chairs, then forgot the number. He kept looking at his watch but the time didn't register. There was a drift of dog-eared magazines on a coffee table. The top one was called *Hello!*.

The consultant came. Mr Thorneycroft. They'd found a tumour on Suzanne's brain. It was operable but brain surgery is always difficult – impossible at this stage to make any meaningful prognosis. She'd be in theatre for several hours, and yes, it might be as well to notify close relatives. A missing daughter? He'd get the social worker to come and have a word.

Mr Thorneycroft left. Time passed. Malcolm flicked through *Hello!* but nothing registered. Nothing went in. A volunteer worker came with tea. She'd just gone when the social worker arrived. Malcolm told him about Annabel, and he mentioned the BBC. An SOS message. Funny, mused Malcolm, I've heard them all my life and never connected them with real people. Actual tragedies. They were just something on the radio, like 'The Archers'.

The social worker said try not to worry. Is there a phone, asked Malcolm, and the social worker said he'd show him. It was Sarah. He must contact Sarah. He didn't have a number for Eden Vale so he'd have to call Neil. He got up and trailed after the social worker. He'd forgotten to drink the tea.

Sixty-Six

Sarah looked up as Deaconess Lynn entered the tent and smiled down at Rebecca and herself. She was Andrew's mother. 'Come along you two – it's time.'

'What's going to happen, Deaconess Lynn?' asked Sarah, getting stiffly to her feet. They'd cowered here all day and she was starving.

'You're going to be purified, child. It's a simple ritual – nothing to be afraid of. Here.' She handed Sarah a long white garment like a very plain nightie. 'Take off your clothes and put this on.'

'Please can we have something to eat first?'

'I'm afraid not. We don't eat while we're unclean. The Pastor is hungry, but he too must wait.'

'A drink of water, then?'

'I'm sorry, no. Hurry, please. You too, Rebecca.'

She looked on as the children changed. 'Leave your clothes on the table,' she said when they were ready, 'and follow me.'

It was dusk outside, and not very warm. They followed the Deaconess towards the middle of the site, their nighties brushing the grass which felt cold under their bare feet. The other children were there, standing in a circle with Deacon Stephen. Fiona's mother didn't seem to be around, and neither did the other parent, Sister Barbara. The Deaconess led them into the centre of the circle. On the ground stood three plastic buckets, brimming with water. Sarah eyed them, hoping the ritual didn't call for one of them to be up-ended over her head. She was freezing as it was.

Presently Pastor Ken emerged from the men's tent. He wore an ankle-length nightie, too, and Sarah had to bite her lip to keep from giggling. He made his way down and joined them in the circle where, without a word, he sank to his knees and bowed his head. Deaconess Lynn signalled to Sarah and Rebecca to do the same, then took Deacon Stephen's place as he moved forward, his arms raised to the darkening sky.

'Dear Lord,' he intoned, 'look down we beseech thee on these your children, whom Satan hath beguiled as the serpent did beguile the woman Eve, and hath rendered them unclean.'

'Hear us, Lord!' cried the onlookers in unison.

'Pity their simplicity, and in Thine infinite mercy grant that they might attain purification by prayer and by water.'

'Hear us, Lord!'

The Deacon lowered his arms and turned towards the kneeling Pastor.

'Brother Pastor – do you detest utterly your unclean state?'

'I do.'

'And do you crave purification by prayer and by water?'

'I do.'

'Remove your garment.'

Remove . . .? Sarah's downcast eyes widened and she caught her lower lip between her teeth. Does that mean . . . when it's my turn will *I* have to . . . in front of all these kids? I don't know if I *can*. Or if I *should*. Oh God – I wish you were here, Mum. I don't know what to *do* . . .

Sixty-Seven

'Is that Neil?'

'Yes. Who's this?'

'Malcolm. Malcolm Henshaw.'

'Ah . . . I've been trying to call *you* but there was no reply.'

'No – I'm at the hospital. My wife's extremely ill and I need to contact Sarah at Eden Vale. Do you have a number?'

'I . . . yes I do, but there's something you ought to know. Can we meet at your house?'

'I don't want to leave the hospital, Neil. Suzanne's in theatre. Can't it wait?'

'I'm afraid not, Malcolm. Your daughter's in the gravest danger. She and the other children.'

'Danger? What sort of danger, for heaven's sake?'

'We can't do this over the phone, Malcolm. I've got somebody with me who'll explain. We'll meet you at your place.'

As he steered the Renault into the kerb, two men came over. Neil nodded towards his companion. 'Malcolm, this is Doctor Alex Partington. He's . . . er . . .'

The man stuck out a hand. 'The tabloids call me a

cult-buster, Mr Henshaw. I investigate religious cults or sects or whatever you want to call them.'

Malcolm nodded. 'Yes, yes . . . I recognise your name from newspaper articles. Can we get to the point, please? I'm anxious to return to the hospital.'

The man nodded. 'I've been looking into the activities of The Little Children and, with the help of Neil here, I've uncovered something extremely unpleasant.'

'But . . .?' Malcolm shook his head. 'There's nothing to uncover, surely? I've attended the meetings. The Bible studies. I never . . . I mean, nothing ever *happened*. Nothing bad. They're just a bunch of ordinary people looking for . . . I don't know . . . some *meaning* in their lives, I suppose. It's not a cult – not what *I'd* call a cult, anyway. Cults have weird rituals, don't they? Orgies, stuff like that.'

'Malcolm.' Neil gripped his arm. 'You've never attended a Faith Camp, have you? *That's* where the weird stuff goes on. It's what the camps are *for*, in fact. That's why your daughter's in danger.'

'But *parents* go, Neil. Mums. Surely they wouldn't let . . .'

Neil gazed at him. 'Ken Caster gets *rid* of 'em, Malcolm. Splits the adults into two groups – the sheep and the goats – and gives them alternate evenings off to eat in town, see a film, whatever.' He shrugged. 'The goats are always the same people.'

The colour drained from Malcolm's cheeks as he stared at the young Deacon. 'Are you . . . are you talking about what I *think* you're talking about?' His voice cracked. 'Because if you are you'd better get in this car right now and take me to Eden Vale.'

Partington interrupted, nodding towards a white Range Rover parked along the road. 'That's mine. You're welcome to come with us if you wish but if you'd rather get back to the hospital, Neil and I will see your daughter safe.'

'You're joking.' Malcolm started towards the vehicle. 'If anything's happened to Sarah . . . anything at all, *somebody's* going to pay. Come *on*.'

Sixty-Eight

Annabel was lying on her bed with a copy of *Just Seventeen* when Mary knocked and stuck her head round the door. Annabel could tell by her expression that something was wrong.

'Annabel?'

'What is it, Mary — what's happened?' She dropped the magazine and sat up, gazing at her friend. Mary sat down on the bed and took her hand.

'I was in the kitchen just now, dear, listening to the radio. There was one of those SOS messages. It was for you.'

Annabel felt herself go cold. 'For me? Are you . . . what did it say?'

'You must go home, Annabel, at once. Your mother is ill in hospital.'

'Ill?' She grabbed Mary's wrist. 'You mean *dangerously* ill, don't you? That's what it said, isn't it? I've heard those messages. They *always* say that.'

Mary nodded. 'Yes, dear, that's what it said, and you must try to stay calm. I'll throw a few things in a bag, we'll take the car and be there in a couple of hours.'

'It's all my fault, isn't it? If I hadn't . . . if . . .' She burst into tears. Mary wrapped her arms round her and murmured in her ear.

'Annabel, don't. Please don't. Of *course* it's not your fault. Your mother has *cancer*. This would have happened no matter what you'd chosen to do, and anyway there isn't *time* for tears. Not now. Here.' She thrust a tissue into the girl's hand. 'Dry your eyes and have a good blow while I see to the bag.'

The SOS message had been broadcast at five past six. At fourteen minutes past, Mary's Micra shot out of the driveway and turned right with a squeal of tyres, heading for the motorway.

Sixty-Nine

'Sister Sarah – do you detest utterly your unclean state?'

I don't know. I can't say no, can I? 'I . . . I do.'

'And do you crave purification by prayer and by water?'

Yes, I want to be pure, of course I do, but it can't be right, can it, Pastor Ken without a stitch on and now me. Why isn't Fiona's mum here, and Sister Barbara? 'I . . . I do.'

'Remove . . .'

Deacon Stephen broke off as a blinding flash split the gloom, followed at once by two more. Children cried out in alarm as shadowy figures moved in the trees, and the circle disintegrated as Deaconess Lynn yelled, 'Run for it, Steve – it's cameras!' They fled, Deacon and Deaconess, across the campsite and into the woods. Pastor Ken leapt to his feet with what sounded to Sarah suspiciously like an oath, snatching up his discarded nightie and holding it in front of him as three men came out of the trees.

'Dad!' Sarah ran to her father, dragging a bewildered Rebecca by the hand. 'Oh, Dad, I'm glad you came. I nearly had to . . .'

He hugged her, then held her at arm's length and peered at her.

'Are you all right, sweetheart? Has anybody . . . touched you?'

She shook her head. 'No, but you have to take everything off and there's this cold water and . . .'

'What about your friend here?'

'Rebecca. She's okay. It wasn't her turn yet. We're unclean, you see.'

'Unclean?'

'From touching ammonites. Satan left them for us to find.'

'No, sweetheart, he didn't. Ammonites are fossilised animals, millions of years old. It was the *Pastor* who left them for you to find.'

'Pastor *Ken*?' Sarah glanced back. The Pastor, still hiding his nakedness with his nightie, was arguing with Deacon Neil while the third new arrival, the man with the camera, seemed to be explaining something to the children. She looked at her father.

'I don't get it, Dad – why would Pastor Ken leave ammonites for us to find? And who's that man, and how did you get here, and why did you come, and how come Deaconess Lynn and Deacon Stephen ran away?'

Her father shook his head. 'It's far too complicated to explain right now, Sarah. For one thing, it turns out Ken Caster's not really a clergyman at all.'

'What *is* he, then?'

'I'll explain later, sweetheart. Right now we've got to get you home – you and the others.'

'How? And what about Fiona's mum and Sister Barbara? They're not here.'

'Don't you worry about them. Look – Neil's getting the kids ready to walk down to the coach. I'm going to ride back with you, because . . .' He sighed. 'I have to talk to you about your Mum.'

Seventy

The Micra slowed. 'Is *this* the gateway, Annabel?'

'No, no – carry on to the next one, please, Mary – this is staff only.'

'Righto.'

The car accelerated briefly, then slowed as Annabel said, 'Here we are.' Mary steered between stone gateposts. A sign pointed the way to the visitors' carpark. She bore right. The car-park was large and floodlit. Mary drove on to it and slotted the Micra into a space, switching off ignition and lights. She sat back with a sigh and looked at her watch. 'Two hours twenty minutes.'

'Thanks, Mary. D'you mind if we . . .?'

'Of *course* not, dear. Come on.'

As they got out, a coach was coming through the gateway. Mary frowned. 'Now why on *earth* would a coachful of kids be visiting a hospital at this time of night?'

Annabel glanced at the vehicle and shrugged. 'Search me.' She didn't care. All she wanted was to find her mother. 'It's this way.' As they set off towards the building the coach turned on to the square and cut across their path before squealing to a halt. Its doors folded back, hissing. Annabel glanced towards it and saw her father coming down the steps. She grabbed Mary's sleeve.

'My . . . my dad.'

'What?' She looked where Annabel was pointing.

'That's my *dad*, Mary. And there's Sarah. DAD!'

Malcolm's head jerked up. He paused on the bottom step, peering at the two figures. Behind him Sarah cried, 'It's *Annabel*, Dad. It *is*!'

'Annabel?' He stepped down and came towards them. 'Is it you?'

'Yes, Dad, it's me. What're you doing on a *coach*? Is Mum . . .?'

'I . . . I don't know. She'll be so happy, though, when . . . if . . . oh, what the heck – let's get *over* there.'

'Okay, Malcolm?' The driver, scrunched down in his seat, peered across at them.

Malcolm waved. 'Okay, Neil, thanks.'

The door hissed shut and the coach rolled forward, turning. Mary gazed after it. 'Neil . . .?' She shook her head. 'No . . . getting silly in my old age, that's what it is.' She turned and hurried after Annabel.

Seventy-One

Dear Mary,

I'm really sorry not to have written before this, but everything here's been so fantastically hectic – I can't believe it's Christmas next week.

First the good news. Mum's home! The operation was a complete success, though she'll have to go back in the New Year for the chemo she missed. She's not very strong, but it'll be lovely to have her with us for Christmas. Dad says we must treasure our time together, and that's what we're doing. I don't think Sarah quite understood what he meant, and that's probably just as well.

Talking of Dad, I'm glad to say he's back to normal. He was really depressed when Ken Caster was arrested and it all came out about The Little Children. There's no God, he kept saying. We're on our own. You should have seen him prowling about the house, muttering. It was almost as bad as his religious phase. I didn't know what to do, so I talked to Mr Bickford at school. [Yes – I'm back in R.E. and Geography and everybody's being very kind.] Anyway, he wrote Dad a long letter which seemed to help, because after he read it he started getting better bit by bit.

Now he says there is a God, and He did create the world, but not as a once-for-all, finished job. He didn't make a sculpture: something in bronze or marble intended to stay the same forever. No. What He made was a garden: something which grows and changes all the time. Ammonites, then dinosaurs, then apemen, then us, then — who knows? Creation's still happening, Dad says. Everything changes. We change. He means the human race. We grow more wise and more kind, and when we come to see the old rules as harsh and cruel we change them. We can't stand still, and we certainly can't go back. [I reckon he got all this from Baldy Bickford, 'cause it just doesn't sound like Dad!] The other day he came out with Evolution is one of God's greatest miracles, so he's certainly changed.

What else? Oh, yes — Sarah. She seems none the worse for her weird experience at Eden Vale. A bit mystified, I think. Dad tried to explain it all to her but I don't think she caught on.

I think that's all my news. Oh — I want to ask a favour, Mary. Another favour, on top of your having befriended me and taken me in and practically saved my life and all that. Next time you're down the shopping centre, would you mind popping into Island and explaining to Mrs North why I never showed up after that one Saturday? She must think I'm awful. Apologise to her for me — please.

Must go. I'm swotting like mad to catch up at school and it's my turn to make the dinner. Write when you get a minute.

Peace and love,

Annabel